blended

ALSO BY SHARON M. DRAPER

Copper Sun
Double Dutch
Out of My Mind
Panic
Romiette & Julio
Stella by Starlight

THE JERICHO TRILOGY
The Battle of Jericho
November Blues
Just Another Hero

THE HAZELWOOD HIGH TRILOGY
Tears of a Tiger
Forged by Fire
Darkness Before Dawn

CLUBHOUSE MYSTERIES
The Buried Bones Mystery
Lost in the Tunnel of Time
Shadows of Caesar's Creek
The Space Mission Adventure
The Backyard Animal Show
Stars and Sparks on Stage

blended

SHARON M. DRAPER

A CAITLYN DLOUHY BOOK

A ATHENEUM BOOKS FOR YOUNG READERS
atheneum New York London Toronto Sydney New Delhi

ATHENEUM BOOKS FOR YOUNG READERS

An imprint of Simon & Schuster Children's Publishing Division

1230 Avenue of the Americas, New York, New York 10020

This book is a work of fiction. Any references to historical events, real people, or real places are used fictitiously. Other names, characters, places, and events are products of the author's imagination, and any resemblance to actual events or places or persons, living or dead, is entirely coincidental.

Text copyright © 2018 by Sharon M. Draper

Jacket illustrations copyright © 2018 by Debra Cartwright

All rights reserved, including the right of reproduction in whole or in part in any form.

ATHENEUM BOOKS FOR YOUNG READERS is a registered trademark of Simon & Schuster, Inc. Atheneum logo is a trademark of Simon & Schuster, Inc.

For information about special discounts for bulk purchases, please contact Simon & Schuster Special Sales at 1-866-506-1949 or business@simonandschuster.com.

The Simon & Schuster Speakers Bureau can bring authors to your live event. For more information or to book an event, contact the Simon & Schuster Speakers Bureau at 1-866-248-3049 or visit our website at www.simonspeakers.com.

Interior design by Irene Metaxatos

Jacket design by Debra Sfetsios-Conover

The text for this book was set in Sabon LT Std.

Manufactured in the United States of America

0918 FFG

First Edition

10 9 8 7 6 5 4 3 2 1

CIP data for this book is available from the Library of Congress.

ISBN 978-1-4424-9500-5

ISBN 978-1-4424-9502-9 (eBook)

This book is dedicated to
all the young people who
must meld and merge,
synthesize and harmonize,
to create family fusion.

blended

CHAPTER 1

PLUNK.
　Plink.
　Ripple.
　Rumble.
　Tinkle.
　Twinkle.
　Boomble. I know that's not an actual word, but it's a real sound. I can create any musical combination of sounds on my piano. That's my superpower.

I sit, hands perched with thirsty fingers, as I get ready to play. I work hard at it, always trying to find the right melodies and harmonies. The upstairs-downstairs scales that rise and fall. The three- and four-finger chords that stomp. The fingernail-delicate tiptoeing up and down the keyboard, each touch a new sound. White keys. Black keys. One at a time. Chords all together. Two keys make a different sound than three played together. Four or five mashed at the same time is even better. I can do nine keys, even ten, to make a chord, but to be honest, that sounds weird.

Each combination at the piano is different. Bass. Treble. Major tones. Minor wails. Bass like a celebration. Treble like tears.

Five-four-three-two-one. One-two-three-four-five. Up. Up. Up. Down. Down. Down. Harmony. Melody. Chords. Scales. The black keys play sad sounds, like somebody crying. The white keys sometimes laugh. Using only my fingers, I can make the black and white keys dance together and do whatever I want.

When I play the piano, I rock! It would be nice if the *rest* of my life came together like some kind of a magical musical symphony. But, nah, not usually.

CHAPTER 2

I STARTED PLAYING piano when I was three. Sort of. For my birthday that year, I got one of those plastic keyboard toys done up in cotton-candy pink, the kind with fat keys that played way out of tune and drove grown-ups crazy. But I loved it. I wasn't interested in any of the dolls or blocks or tea sets I'd been given, only that piano—plinking and plunking on it nonstop. My parents had to take it away from me that night, just for a little quiet, and I cried myself to sleep. The next morning I demanded they take it down from the top of the refrigerator, where they'd put it out of my reach, and I played on it most of the rest of the day.

I learned to pick out tunes, figured out the different tones of each note. I wanted more.

So my big Christmas ask was always for a piano. Top of my list. Even though my parents would tease me and pretend they'd forgotten, every other year I'd find a big box wrapped in red paper. A toy piano. A red one. Another pink one. Each one a little better than the one before. I taught myself to create my own tunes and, later, to read a little music. Yeah, I was obsessed. But still, they were just toys, and usually some of the plastic keys would give out in a few months.

The Christmas after I turned seven, there was no big box at all. I got a doll, which they should have known I was no longer interested in, some clothes, a few art supplies for painting and drawing, and a couple of board games, which was dumb because we didn't usually sit down and play anything together as a family. I suppose it was selfish, but I was kinda mad.

Finally, after all the gifts had been opened, Mom said, all chipper, "I'm hungry. Let's have pancakes!"

Daddy said, just as cheery, "Good idea! Isabella, would you check to see if we have pancake mix?"

I couldn't figure out why he was asking me to do that, but it was Christmas, so I said sure. I checked the cupboard, actually found *two* boxes of the mix, and returned to the living room to report.

Sitting in the middle of the floor, where just moments ago there'd been only balled-up red-and-green paper, was a *huge* box wrapped in silver.

On it was my name written in large black letters. I gasped.

"Open it!" my parents said together.

I hesitated just for a second, then tore through the wrapping. It was a portable piano. A *real* piano keyboard—a Casio!

"Oh, wow!" I remember saying.

It was black and shiny and seemed to fill up the whole living room floor. I was in heaven.

With eighty-eight weighted keys, it almost felt like a real piano. Built-in speakers, too, plus buttons I could push for rhythms like jazz beats and military and drums. I didn't really need those, but they added fun. I could record on it and play back stuff I'd created. It let me listen to myself, so I could correct mess-ups and smooth out the hard sections.

Mom signed me up for piano lessons at school. Daddy bought me sheet music. But even though my parents were the ones who'd bought it for me, they started getting annoyed at my constant banging on that Casio. Some days they looked angry when they told me to "give it a break," and it took me a while to realize they weren't really mad at me, but at each other. The noise probably jangled their nerves. And their nerves were plenty jangled—they had always fought about stupid stuff, but now it seemed like they fought All. The. Time.

They bickered over whether we'd have hot dogs or hamburgers for dinner. They squabbled over whether I should wear jeans or leggings. An argument could break out at any moment—over lost car keys or bars of soggy soap or burned toast. Then there was the Kool-Aid incident—who woulda thought something as simple as Kool-Aid would cause a fight? But yeah. That was about three years ago—I guess I was around eight.

They started arguing right before dinner. Daddy hated blue Kool-Aid for some reason. He said the turquoise color and the raspberry flavor just didn't make sense, so he wouldn't drink it. I was sitting at the table, getting ready to pour myself a big glass of it. Mom's voice got loud. Daddy's voice got louder.

By this point, I was shaking. Really shaking. Then Daddy actually started shouting, and I dropped the entire container of the stuff on the floor. The pitcher broke. Blue, sticky mess went everywhere. And the shouting turned to bellows and Mom started crying, and I knew I was in so much trouble!

I ran to my room, curled on my bed, and covered my ears with a pillow.

When the hollering finally settled down, it was way past my bedtime. I tiptoed into the kitchen and grabbed two slices of cold pizza from the refrigerator. Mom and Daddy had forgotten about dinner and, apparently, about me.

CHAPTER 3

I WAS JUST getting up the next morning when Daddy knocked on my door.

"You 'wake?" he asked gently.

"Yeah."

"You okay?"

"I guess." I sat up against my pillow.

"I'm sorry, Isabella. I'm so very sorry that the problems between me and your mom get all mixed into your life."

"Mom was crying," I told him. I'm not sure if I was accusing him or wanting an explanation. Probably both.

"I know. I guess all I can tell you is how sorry I am" was all he said.

"I'm sorry I spilled the Kool-Aid. I made a mess. . . . And I know sometimes I forget to wash the dishes."

"No, no, no!" he said quickly. "You've done *nothing* wrong. Not one thing. And it was *our* fault, not yours! We were being ugly to each other, and you shouldn't have had to hear it. I'm so sorry. None of this is about a drink that has too much sugar in it." He gave me a little hug and a smile. "The Kool-Aid was just the thing we disagreed about this time. It could have been the carpet, the toothpaste, even the weather—we just can't seem to agree about anything anymore."

"Uh, yeah. I've noticed," I said in sort of a mumble. "It's kinda hard not to."

Daddy traced my nose with his finger. "We argue about lots of stuff, but never about you, Isabella. *That* we both agree on. We both absolutely adore *you*! You understand that, right?"

It was clear he wanted me to say yes, so I nodded.

"Your mom is upset with *me*, Izzy, not you," Daddy went on.

Weird. Daddy hardly ever called me that. It was Mom's nickname for me. He liked the sound of

"Isabella" when he said it out loud, he'd always say. "None of this is your fault."

"So why are you two always yelling and mad at each other?"

He nodded like I'd asked a smart question. He nodded for so long I wondered if he'd forgotten what I actually asked. Then he said, "Because . . . because, uh, we've kinda ended up growing in different directions."

I pressed my lips together, hard. This didn't sound like a good thing. So I told him, "But you're grown-ups! You're already done growing!"

"I'm so sorry," he said again. It made me kinda itchy, listening to my daddy keep apologizing to me. Somehow that just didn't feel right either. Then he started sniffling.

"Sweetheart, the thing is . . . I've been unhappy for such a long time. So has your mom. The frustrations just piled up. . . . It's just not working anymore." Daddy was blinking hard.

What wasn't working? Our *family*? Because of frustrations, he'd said. I gulped; I'd caused lots of frustrations! A couple of weeks ago I burned the cupcakes I was making because I forgot to set the timer. I lost my math homework and Mom had to call the teacher. And twice last week I forgot to flush the toilet—ick. What was *wrong* with me?

"Is it *my* fault?" I blurted out.

"Oh, no, no, no, no, no!" he cried, reaching for me. "Isabella, you are absolutely, one hundred percent perfect! It's us, not you." He paused then and looked me straight in the eye. His face was so close that I could see a couple of beard hairs he'd missed when he shaved. "I want you to understand that your mom and I love you very, very much."

I waited. I could tell there was a "but" coming—a reason, an explanation, an excuse. And it came, the worst "but" ever.

"But we have decided that it would be better if I went to live in another house so that we can stop all this fighting."

I shook his hand from my shoulder. "You're moving out?"

I couldn't even make my mouth say words. "To . . . to . . . where?"

He looked down, traced the pattern of my bedspread with his finger. Then he said something even *worse.* "Isabella, I've been offered a job in California."

"California!" I jumped off the bed and glared at him. "That's a million miles away from Ohio! How will I . . . ? When will I . . . ?" And I couldn't finish either question 'cause I knew I'd start bawling.

"You can visit every summer. And at Christmas. And spring break. And I will *always* be here for you, baby girl. Always." He tried to sound positive, but it sure sounded like a load of fake to me.

"Parents like to say stuff like that," I told him, balling my hands into fists—open, closed, open, closed. "But if you live in California, Daddy, you won't be here for my piano recitals or . . . or . . . my soccer games! You *won't* 'always be here' for me!"

Daddy started with the nodding thing again. "Uh, there's FaceTime and video chats and all that computer stuff you kids are so good at. You can show me. We'll stay in constant contact. Every day. I *promise*."

Those tears in his eyes were getting ready to fall. No! *He* was not the one who should be crying, even if he did look like the saddest dad on Earth right now.

So I said, "Pinkie swear?" to make him feel better, even though this felt way too big for a little old pinkie.

He offered me his left hand—strong and brown. I offered him mine—soft and pale. My hand was trembling. But then I pulled away suddenly. I had to ask him one more question. All the whispers and giggles and stifled remarks I'd heard at school kinda flooded my mind. Stuff I'd ignored or brushed off. I had to ask. I had to know.

"Daddy, are you and Mommy splitting up because you're Black and she's white?"

He got real serious. He circled my face with his hands—so gently. Then he whispered, "No, my precious Isabella. This has nothing to do with race. Please believe me. When your mom and I first met, we simply fell in love. We didn't see color—she saw *me*. I saw *her*. And for a while, that was enough. . . . You've gotta believe that." His eyes seemed to be pleading for me to understand.

I said nothing for a minute, staring at him a long time, trying to memorize every inch of his cocoa brown face; his wide shoulders; his thick, black hair. Slowly I offered him my pinkie finger again.

"I pinkie swear that I will love you forever," he said, almost in tears.

I bit down on my lip. No crying. No.

"Me too" is what I said. I didn't add that the idea of a forever without my daddy seemed to me like music without sound.

CHAPTER 4

AT FIRST THE word "divorce" scared me. It was like our family had come down with a horrible, incurable disease or something. Like that Kool-Aid pitcher, we were shattered, and my parents couldn't fix whatever was wrong.

I was stupid sad after Dad left. I looked at a map of the United States at school. The distance from Ohio to California was *so* huge—he coulda been on another planet. It would take three days just to drive there! But even if he had just moved across town, he was gone from *me*. I couldn't see him or sit in his lap when I wanted to or needed to.

And never mind what he said, deep inside I *did* feel like it was partly my fault. I'd messed up a lot. The Kool-Aid. The cupcakes. Then there was the time they'd given me a necklace after my first piano recital—it was a shiny musical note on a silver chain. Mom had warned me not to wear it to soccer practice, but I didn't listen. It fell off on the field somewhere and I couldn't find it. They said they were disappointed in me. That made my stomach hurt. So yeah, I really was one big frustration.

During those first few weeks after Dad left, I spent the days walking around what was now the house for just me and Mom, touching all the "Dad places": the green kitchen chair—the one that didn't wobble; the empty bathroom shelf where he used to keep his aftershave that smelled like peppermint patties; the old pottery ashtray where he used to toss his keys.

After dinner I would carefully wash his favorite plate—the blue ceramic one—even though it hadn't been used, just so it wouldn't get dusty. I'd put it back in the cupboard next to that big red bowling plate he'd won a couple of years ago. I don't know why he didn't take those when he moved out, but I was glad they were still there, 'cause maybe that meant he might come back, right?

Plus, Mom's place was just so *quiet* all the time. So I hauled out my Casio again and again, just to make some noise.

When my parents finally got official custody papers with legal instructions from a judge, I guess that sealed everything. We were no longer a whole, but three separate pieces. A mom. A dad. A kid sliced in half. Actually, that made us *four* pieces—'cause I have to be two people: Mom's Izzy and Dad's Isabella.

But even though I got to go to the beach whenever I visited him, and even though Dad's California house was awesome—with a big old Steinway piano he got just for me—I always felt like a visitor. Which I was. I only *visited* him. Daddy wasn't . . . home. But I got used to it. What choice did I have?

The system worked, basically, until last year. When Dad decided to move again. And suddenly he was just across town.

And now that he's once again living in the same city as I do, the custody rules have changed. It took a little getting used to. Okay, truth? It took a *lot* of getting used to.

CHAPTER 5

DAD LIVES IN a really nice house now that he's back, and I mean *ridiculously* nice—the kind of house you see on TV shows about movie stars. It's in a ritzy suburb just outside of town.

Mom still lives in the small house we all used to share. It's crisp and clean and usually smells like the candle fragrance she bought that week. Last week she was burning a lavender-lime—a purple-green swirled combination that actually smelled really good. She got it at Target. I wish I'd been with her.

But unless we're doing a custody exchange, it's never the three of us together anymore. Probably never ever again.

When Dad moved back, and he and Mom went to court so a new custody arrangement could be worked out, I was not allowed to go. Excuse me, but I think I should have had a say in it, especially since the whole thing was about *me* anyway. But I didn't.

Right before the court date, I spent one whole Saturday night on my laptop, researching custody laws in Ohio. Mom is my legal guardian because she's, like, my mom. But she and Dad have shared custody of me, which means they have to take turns. But I have no "legal right to choose." That's a real phrase from a custody article I looked up. Makes me feel pretty small. Some judge who had never even met me decided to split me in half. Like that's even humanly possible.

So I live with Dad and Anastasia—Dad's "lady friend," as he calls her—and her son, Darren, one week. Then, every Sunday, at exactly 3:00 p.m., in front of the Apple Store at the mall, I am exchanged like a wrong-size pair of jeans. And I live with Mom and her boyfriend, John Mark, the next week. Yeah, they love me and all that, but it doesn't stop them from slicing my life in half every seven days and then acting like that's normal or something.

Every Monday I wake up in a different bed than the one I slept in the week before.

I *hate* that!

Birds make nests in trees, right? One nest. One tree. Who ever heard of a robin moving her eggs every week to a new tree? That'd be crazy, right?

Yep. Crazy.

Welcome to my life.

CHAPTER 6
Mom's Week

JOHN MARK METZKER has been around longer than the other six guys Mom sorta dated, whose names I choose not to remember. Before I got to know him, I used to call him simply Number Seven, but not to his face. After a couple of years, it was clear that he and Mom really liked each other. And I can tell he really likes me. He's honest, real polite, and he likes crunchy peanut butter and apricot jelly—never grape—just like I do.

Mom smiles, sometimes even giggles, when she's around him, and I can see a little of the tired, pinched look leave her face when he comes into a room. I like that he makes her happy.

He's a red neck. I don't mean that in a negative way. But he seriously has a sunburn-red neck. He keeps sun block on the kitchen counter and slathers it on each morning before he leaves the house. He keeps his hair cut short, so there really is no protection for his poor neck. I'd never met a person who really had skin like that, one of those people who fry at the beach—honest! He's the only guy I know who cooks like a Pop-Tart in the sun, but he's pretty cool. He laughs a lot, loves to sing, blushes a lot, is a little overweight, and I've never seen him in a bad mood. He's got dozens of interesting tattoos—it's fun to "read" his arms during the summer when he wears short-sleeved shirts.

When he gets in his truck, he turns the country-western station up as loud as it will go, then sings along with folks like Willie Nelson and Garth Brooks. He says he likes the oldies, whatever that means.

He really likes my mom.

CHAPTER 7
Exchange Day

IT'S SUNDAY. I hate Sundays. I hate, hate, hate them. Even when I'm a wrinkled old lady, Sunday will always remind me of a worn, gray fake-leather sofa at the mall. It's where Dad sits to wait for me when it's his turn for custody for the week. Mom waits on the same couch on the opposite week. The stupid sofa never changes— just the faces of the grown-ups who come to claim me. I'm pretty sure my parents hate Sundays too.

Today, Dad waits stiffly, tapping his fingers, like he can't relax until this is over. Probably true! He is never late. Anastasia sits beside him. She, at least, is smiling. Her shoes and purse are probably real leather—very fancy looking. She's dressed in an amber-tone wool suit that's almost the same color she is. Probably took her hours to do her face and hair. I touch the fuzzy frizz I call mine; it's bushed out of the scrunchie. Again.

But today I break into a wide smile as Mom and I approach them, because Anastasia's son, Darren, has come with them. He's . . . well, not to sound like a fan girl, but he's totally cool. He knows how to dress so he looks really sharp without looking like he worked at it, and he's got a gravelly sounding voice that makes my friends get all kinds of silly.

I glance back guiltily at Mom, who is pale and tired looking, trying to scrape a stain off her Waffle House uniform with her fingernail. John Mark, in his favorite blue bowling shirt, walks on the other side of me. They're speed-walking because we are late. Again. I wonder if other people are watching us, like we're some kind of reality TV show. The caption would read: "Chocolate family meets vanilla family in the artificial reality that is a mall. Caramel daughter caught helplessly between the two."

When we get to the sofa, Mom simply nods curtly at my father and Anastasia, gives me a forehead kiss, then turns and hurries away with John Mark. Dad nods as well. No need to exchange words, just me. They've got that head-nodding thing down to a science.

Now he hops up and I step into his outstretched arms. "What's up, my Bella Isabella?" He smooths my hair. He's been calling me that since I was little—it's from a picture book that I used to make him read to me over and over. I couldn't believe that someone had written about a girl—a warrior princess—with my name. I still have that book.

"I'm great, Daddy," I tell him, then I quickly let go and grab Darren's arm.

"I'm so glad you came today! What's up?"

"I decided to witness the exchanging of the captive," he teases, grabbing my backpack and slinging it over his shoulder. "Besides, I had to get my phone fixed."

"How's *Aleeesha*?" I ask, my turn to tease. "I hardly saw you the last time I was there."

"If you must know," he says, poking me in the arm, "Alicia is so very yesterday! I'm working up the courage to ask Monique to the dance next week."

"I bet she's checking her phone every hour in case you text!"

"Maybe," he says, his voice a mystery.

"Still living up there on the honor roll?"

"Is there anywhere else?" He rolls his eyes.

"How's Miss Pearson at the homeless shelter?"

"Still passing out mashed potatoes, blankets, and goody bags."

"I've got some of those little lotion and shampoo bottles in my bag for her," I tell him. "I saw them at CVS on sale for fifty cents each the other day, so I bought a bunch to help Miss Pearson out."

"You're the best, Izzy."

"I know!" I tell him as I play punch him in the side.

Here's the scoop on Darren. He's totally awesome. In addition to volunteering at the homeless shelter, he gets grades that land him on the honor roll every quarter. He runs the fastest 100-meter dash on the track team. He's got a boatload of colleges writing him letters, asking him to consider their university. *They* are asking *him*. Yeah, pretty impressive.

Best thing? He buys me ice cream every time I ask, even if it's before dinner. Like I said—he's the total package.

I go to Anastasia next and give her a hug as well. She's a good hugger—it feels real, not faked. She smells like Shalimar—it's a fancy French perfume I've learned to really like.

"So good to see you again, Isabella," she murmurs. "I've missed you." And she means it.

CHAPTER 8
Mom's Week

WHIPLASH. THAT'S WHAT it feels like when I'm on a ride at the amusement park and it stops real fast. Last summer, Mom took me to the Hamilton County Fair. I loved it—the Tilt-A-Whirl and the Dragon Tail and the Racing Rollers—coasters on a double track! Best Saturday ever!

Then it was over. Like this week—I'm at Mom's. I feel comfy when I'm here. Then the week is over. And I'm with Dad. I gotta get comfortable again in another house with different food and clothes and rules and stuff. It gets to be a pain. A weekly whiplash.

At least I don't have to change schools every

time. Lakeview Mountain School is halfway between my parents' houses. There is no lake nearby, no mountain, no view of anything much except houses and apartment buildings. It's big—we've got grades five through eight. Fifth graders look like scared little mice at the beginning of the school year. Did I look like that last year? They grow up to be eighth graders who remind me of sumo wrestlers, but we know to keep out of their way.

I like the cafeteria, though. They've tried to set it up so it almost looks like a real restaurant, and the food is only half bad. Today I plop my stuff next to Heather and Imani, who are already munching away.

"What's up, girl?" Imani asks.

"Nothin'," I reply as I grab one of her chips. Imani is tall and slim and dark, like some kind of African princess from a movie. She wears her hair in an Afro on purpose. It's neat and black and perfectly round. Mine, on the other hand, is thick and frizzy with brownish-gold strands that can escape from every scrunchie ever made. The hair spray that can hold it down has not yet been invented. Yeah. Lucky me.

Imani dances ballet. She's really limber and can fold herself into something that looks like a pretzel. When she walks, it's almost like she glides. Boys trail behind her in silence and gawk. She ignores them.

Nobody looks at me like that.

Heather, with hair I can only describe as tangerine colored (I'm for real), once told me she thought her hair made her look like she was wearing a pizza. "Ick," I'd told her. "Give yourself some credit, girl. You're a fashion flame!"

"Hey, I like that," she'd replied, faking a runway pose.

Heather usually brown-bags her lunch—her mom insists on packing healthy stuff like apples and carrot sticks. But as I look at the spaghetti goo I picked up from the food line, her lunch looks pretty good. And we always end up sharing whatever chips Imani brings.

After lunch we take our time leaving the cafeteria before heading to English class, where Mr. Kazilly awaits.

As we pass a table full of sixth-grade boys, I throw out there, in a low voice, "Have you ever seen anybody with eyes as green as Clint Hammond's?"

"Or a face as goofy as Logan Lindquist's?" Heather adds. She makes fun of him, but I know she's scrawled his name over and over and over again on the last page of her English notebook. Capital $\mathcal{L}$ is her favorite letter.

Heather boldly bumps into their table, jiggling it. The boys look up, then pretend they didn't. I turn around just in time to see Logan toss a french fry right at us. It lands in Heather's hair.

She pulls it out and cracks up. She does *not* throw it away, I notice.

Toby Smythe, who, by the way, is wearing a sleeveless athletic jersey even though it's the middle of January, raises both his arms in the air, makes a stupid roaring noise, then sits back down. His buddies, including Clint and Logan, give him high fives.

Now *we* act like we didn't see anything. But as soon as we get into the hall, Heather says, "Ew—did you see Toby's got long, dangly underarm hair?"

Imani nods. "Totally gross."

"Clint is still the cutest," I say shyly.

"For sure," Imani agrees. "Best-looking, uh, white boy in the sixth grade."

I'm not sure what to say to that, but she and I kinda look at each other. Of course I know that Clint is white. I've just never *thought* about it, him being white. I swallow hard.

Then Heather adds, "Except for maybe . . ."

"Logan Lindquist!" we all say in unison.

CHAPTER 9
Mom's Week

MR. KAZILLY, WHO teaches us both English and history, is a certified crazy man, at least in our opinion. He wears UGGS every day—even in the summer. I bet his feet totally stink at the end of the day!

His clothes are, well, let me describe them. He wears stuff like maroon capes and turquoise slacks, or stiff-collared button-down shirts with pinstripes. He's got huge muscles, and he boasts about how he works out at the gym after school. He's one of those people who might get noticed by a fashion magazine, maybe under the category of "Distinctive Teacher Style" or in an athletic magazine under the heading "Teachers with

Six-Packs." He likes colors—he calls them "hues"—so he might wear lavender and chartreuse together, partly for fashion, but I swear he dresses funky so we can have new vocabulary words.

Word. The man is a vocab freak. Ha, ha—get it? Word—vocabulary? Never mind. Anyway. This week's words? A bunch of ordinary ones, like "mischief" and "possibility," but he threw two cool ones in there: "collywobbles" and "gardyloo."

Logan Lindquist raises his hand. "Why we ever gonna need words like this?" he asks.

"To broaden your language skills," Mr. K. says in that reasonable, patient teacher voice.

Without missing a beat, Logan hollers, "I'm feeling kinda collywobbles, sir. I gotta hurl!" He runs to the garbage can, picks it up, and pretends to gag and vomit.

Of course the class cracks up.

And, of course, Mr. Kazilly is not amused. He opens his mouth to shut Logan up, when Logan suddenly hollers, "Gardyloo!" and slings the contents of the wastebasket across the front of the room. Balled-up papers and potato chip wrappers and empty juice boxes fly everywhere!

Chaos. Shock. Laughter.

Logan gets an hour of detention. "Totally worth it!" he says with an arm pump to his friend Toby of the Hairy Armpits. In Logan's defense, I'm sure none of us will *ever* forget the meaning of those two words.

When Mr. Kazilly tells us our homework assignment, however, he's got *me* wanting to shout "gardyloo" and chuck the wastebasket across the room. We have to write an essay called "The Real Me."

Heather and Imani both raise their hands. They always ask the questions I haven't got the nerve to.

Mr. Kazilly nods toward Heather. She gets called on all the time.

"So why do we have to write this *now*?" she asks in her most polite-for-the-teacher voice. "This seems more like a getting-to-know-you paper for, like, when school first starts in the fall."

I shrink in my seat, just in case the teacher decides to blow fire from his nostrils like a dragon.

But he's cool with the question. "I want each of you to consider your personal identity as we begin the new year. Each of you is uniquely wonderful. I want you to think about that as you write." He's, like, beaming as he says this. I bet he spent his whole holiday vacation thinking this one up.

Heather gives me the *you gotta be kidding me*

bug-eye. I cover my mouth to keep from laughing.

"Your paper is due on Monday," Mr. Kazilly says. "At least four paragraphs." The whole class groans, but he's good at ignoring us. He never gets around to calling on Imani.

For me, I gotta remember that I'll start the essay at Mom's house and turn it in while I'm at Dad's.

This assignment totally sucks. The real me? I have no idea who that is. Especially since there's pretty much *two* of me.

CHAPTER 10
Mom's Week

The Real Me

My name is Isabella Badia Thornton. Isabella is an awesome name—it flows like the music of a waterfall. I gotta admit, though, when I think of a character in a book named Isabella, she's tall, got blue eyes, and has long, flowing pale-gold hair. Well, actually, that kinda describes my mom.

But that blue-eyed princess is so not me. My skin is kinda bronze-colored, I guess. I'm not real tall, my eyes are a deep green color, and my hair is wild and kinky—

and kind of a dirty brown. If I'm reading a book about a girl named Isabella, I figure at some point she's going to walk on a golden sandy beach where the wind is blowing so that her perfect blond hair can "billow in the breeze." I've read that line in stories. Clearly, none of those writers have met me. Or my hair. Ha!

My father gave me the middle name Badia. It's African, and it means "unique" or "unprecedented." I like that. He told me that he and Mom had their first argument on the day I was born. She didn't want me to be "bogged down" by what she called "some crazy African name," but Dad insisted. And he was right—when I say my middle name out loud, it lifts me up. I stand a little taller. When I'm a famous pianist, I'll make sure the name written in fancy script on the program says my full name—Isabella Badia Thornton. It is who I am.

CHAPTER 11
Dad's Week

MY FATHER, ISAIAH Maxwell Thornton III, landed a position as a lawyer at the biggest bank in town when he moved back. He specializes in complicated banking cases—"investment banking," I've heard him say. I'm not exactly sure what that means, but I do know all the money he deals with belongs to somebody else. I figure he must be good at his job, though, because he always has a lot of cash to spend on me.

He drives a brand-new black Mercedes with all the frills. Man, that car sure does smell good! The seats are so soft they sorta hug you. We *never* eat french fries in Dad's car.

He likes to dress up. Three-piece suits. Crisp white button-downs. Cuff links that match his ties. Buttoned down and buttoned up—that's my dad. I feel like he's more comfortable dressed like that. He once wore a suit when we went bowling. No joke. I made him take off the tie and the jacket and roll up his sleeves.

"This isn't the opera, Daddy—why are you always so *proper*?" I asked him when he picked me up from school one day.

He gave me a look, but he loosened his tie. "I thought we might stop by Target," he said instead. "I know you like that place, and you might want to get a T-shirt or some jeans or something."

"Yeah, that would be cool," I told him. "But you gotta learn to chill, Dad. Maybe you can get something like ordinary clothes for yourself while we're there. You look like you're the president of the company or something!" I gave him the sad sad sad headshake. So he completely took off the tie. But he couldn't bring himself to wrinkle his shirt by rolling up the sleeves. Pitiful.

Mom, on the other hand, has a dozen pairs of leggings, three well-worn pairs of jeans, and probably a million cool T-shirts. She likes shirts that have clever sayings. Last week she wore one that said, "Teach

your kids about taxes—eat 30% of their ice cream!"
They always make me laugh.

Dad *will* wear a shirt without a collar, and even
jeans on weekends, but he sends them to the cleaner's,
so there's a crease down the center of each leg, like
Sunday pants. Yep. Pitiful times two.

"And by the way, Daddy, you gotta stop ironing
your jeans! Nobody does that!" I told him as we
walked from the car toward the giant red circle Target
sign. He just laughed.

Then he looked at my torn, frayed jeans. "And
you think *those* are a fashion statement?" he asked,
smirking.

"Yep. They even sell them here. And they're not
cheap!" I reminded him with a laugh of my own.

"Hmm. You look . . . impoverished."

"And that's bad?"

"For my daughter, yeah." His face grew serious.
"Here's the thing. I think it's important we look our
very best at all times."

"We, like you and me?" I asked, even though I
knew what he really meant.

He sucked his breath in slowly. "No, Isabella. Like
us, like people of color, like Black folks. *That* we."

I cocked my head. "Why?"

It took him a few clicks before he finally said, "The world looks at Black people differently. It's not fair, but it's true."

I was already aware of this, but I didn't think Dad had ever been so direct about it. Mom for sure would never have had this conversation with me.

So I flat out asked: "Does the world look at *me* that way?"

He answered without hesitation. "Yes."

"But what about the Mom half of me?"

"To me, that's probably the best half of you, the part that makes you smart and funny and lovable and just plain cute!" he told me with a big smile. "But it has *nothing* to do with skin color or race. And everything to do with the flavor of Kool-Aid you turned out to be. You understanding what I'm sayin'?"

I nodded.

Then his face got serious again. "But the world can't see the inside of a person. What the world *can* see is the color."

The doors of Target opened with a welcoming swoosh, and I was instantly distracted. Yeah. Target does that to me. I feel at home. They've got stuff I need. Stuff I don't need. Stuff I didn't even know I wanted. Neatly placed and waiting for me. I love that place. I was trying to handle what Imani calls "all the feels" I was getting right then.

Dad was oblivious to the "feels" and kept on talking. "For instance, did you know there are people in this store—in all department stores, actually—who walk around looking like ordinary customers but are really security police making sure no one is stealing?"

"For real?" I looked around. There was an old lady with a shopping cart full of cat food and three tennis rackets. Maybe she was one! Or that bearded guy who was carrying one of those red baskets. He was buying Cheerios and Coke. *Dude, you need some milk!*

Dad put his hand on my shoulder. "And even though it's not fair, Black folks are followed more often than others. A friend of mine filed a lawsuit a few years ago for a young man—for this very thing."

I slowed down. I felt like my head was popping, the Target magic fading a little. "Well, we shouldn't shop here anymore!" I declared, as if my few dollars would make a difference.

"Won't matter. Like I said, every single department store and grocery store—even the dollar store—has security personnel."

"I just never thought of that," I said, fury building inside me. "Well . . . well . . . then I'll never shop again!"

He just gave me his *You are crazy, girl* look. "Ha! Not my Isabella, the shopping queen! She'll be back."

So, yeah, kinda sad, I knew he was pretty much right. I *loved* this place. I pulled the cart to a full stop near the sporting goods department. Everything was so neatly displayed. There were rackets and rods, balls and bats, and even ropes—for jumping Double Dutch or lassoing cattle, I guess. That made me giggle. I didn't even *need* a batting helmet, but I saw one that was so cute I actually wanted to buy it! Yep, Target's got it goin' on.

We wandered around the store, Dad letting me choose anything I wanted. I got a couple of T-shirts for myself, and one for Mom that said, "My favorite child gave me this shirt!" Dad either didn't mind or didn't notice—he made no comment. I also picked up some hair gel and scrunchies, and a new pair of sneakers—gold ones! Imani and Heather would love them. I was looking, but I couldn't spot anybody who might be secret security.

I wondered if my mom ever thought about this kind of stuff when she shopped. Probably not. She's got that stupidly perfect, straight, honey-gold hair and is pale and incredibly pretty—random people have stopped her to ask if she's a model. Nobody has ever asked me that! I can tell it makes her feel good when that happens, though. Even though she looks away, her smile tells me.

I bet she's the type of person security folks are trained *not* to follow.

CHAPTER 12
Mom's Week

I MAKE IT my goal to practice on my Casio every single day this week, either at Mom's house or at Waffle House.

I'm getting ready for a huge piano recital called Pianopalooza—I wonder if the person who thought of that name had too much coffee that morning. But it's serious—a chance for lots of young musicians like me to show off their skills. It's supposed to be low stress, but of course all the parents and teachers freak out about it. So then it becomes high stress. The planners call it family friendly. I guess that could be true, if your families are actually friendly to each other!

It seems like a long time away, but the recital will be here before I know it. It's gonna be held the second Saturday in June at the University of Cincinnati. It will fall on a Dad week. The university is a really huge place. Inside that big old university is the College-Conservatory of Music. And that's where you find Werner Recital Hall.

Getting to perform there is a *really* big deal.

I sat in the very back one time when Dad took me to a concert by some famous Polish pianist. There's a performance-quality piano on the stage—with really loud speakers hooked up to it. And rows and rows and rows of seats—about a hundred fifty of them. The walls and floors are lined with old-time gleaming wood, and the sound is amazing.

Every perfect note a student plays rings out like a clear crystal bell.

And every mistake echoes like thunder.

CHAPTER 13
Mom's Week

WHEN JOHN MARK picks me up from school on Friday, he seems to be in a really good mood. He drives this monster-huge Ford truck, the kind where if another guy driving a monster-huge truck pulls up beside him, they both start all nodding at each other and revving their engines. On his radio somebody named Dolly Parton is belting out a country song about some love gone wrong, but John Mark is all smiles.

"How 'bout we go rolling and knock down some pins?" he asks as I click in my seat belt. "Your mom is off early tonight and there's no school tomorrow."

"Sounds good," I tell him. John Mark is the manager of Scatterpin Lanes, so I get lots of chances to up my game. "Sounds . . . like it's right up my alley!"

He groans. "Spare me the weak jokes!"

"'*Spare* me'?" I hit back, slapping my forehead. "I'm getting ready to go all the way—nothin' but strikes!"

"Who you talkin' to?" he replies, puffing his chest. "When I throw a turkey, don't start shakin'!"

"You might throw eight in a row," I shoot back, "but can you finish?" I put my hands on my hips—sort of. The seat belt cramps my style.

"Be afraid, 'cause I'm rolling eight!" he tells me as we drive to Scatterpin Bowl.

"Eight gutter balls!"

"Let's go hit 'em!" he roars. His face is bright pink with laughter.

"I hear the bowling thunder," I tell him, "and my lightning is about to strike you down!"

Yep, bowling humor. Gotta love it.

When we get there, Mom's already all set up. She's ordered mozzarella sticks for me, a pizza for the three of us, and Cokes all around. Zeke, the assistant manager, waves and gives us a thumbs-up. I run back to John Mark's office, grab my ball and shoes, and hurry back out to the lanes.

I was teasing John Mark about the bowling thunder, but I gotta admit, I really do love this—the balls whizzing down the oiled wooden lanes, the sound of the pins falling, and the cheers or groans of folks who got that strike or ended up with a gutter ball.

Mom's totally into it too. She has a surprisingly strong arm swing. She throws straight and true, and her delivery is, like, lethal. Me, I'm still learning, but John Mark says if I played in a league with other kids my age, I'd destroy them.

When it's my turn, Mom's got my back. "Quit throwing baby balls!" she cries. "Blow a rack, Izzy! You can do it!"

"Come on, Izzy!" John Mark joins in as I take my stance. "You got this!"

"Ten in the pit, Izzy!" Mom cries. "Smash the pocket!"

I pull my arm back, swing it forward, and let the ball go. Whoa! Perfectly aligned with the center arrows! I am unstoppable!

"Awesome, Izzy!" John Mark yells. "A perfect pocket shot—right in the center, kiddo!"

"Strike!" Mom cheers. "Again! Woo-hoo! That's my baby!" The pins fall with a resounding clatter.

I dab, all proud. "I am ah-ma-zing!" I crow to whoever's around to hear.

As Mom takes her turn, I check out all the folks there—the mother who's letting her kid have a bowling birthday party, the league players in their matching orange or blue or purple striped shirts, and the couples on dates, taking turns and intently checking each other out as the other one bowls.

I watch the lady with bright-pink leggings that are way too tight and a family of six dressed exactly alike in red-and-black pajamas. To my left is a balding man who is bowling with an even older gray-haired woman—his mom, maybe? I cheer for the little kid with a tiny child-size ball who finally hits a pin, and try not to stare at the man with so many tattoos that I can't see his natural skin. John Mark's got bunches of tattoos, but this dude's tats make his look like kindergarten drawings.

I breathe deep. It smells like fun in here. Like family. Like happiness. And pizza, of course.

It's late when we finally leave. John Mark had the highest score, as usual. But I edged out Mom by seven pins. And I don't think she let me win either.

CHAPTER 14
Exchange Day

AFTER THE GREAT Exchange, Dad, Anastasia, Darren, and I take our time ambling down the mall toward the Cheesecake Factory, where we have our every-other-Sunday feast. The servers know us by name.

I order the four-cheese pasta, which is like mac and cheese all maxed out, and a small Cobb salad because Anastasia insists I eat something green and healthy. I always get the banana cream cheesecake for dessert. It's crazy good.

While we wait for our food, Anastasia and Dad are going on and on, all excited, because Darren has an interview next week with Harvard! Even I know that's a huge deal. Plus, Anastasia just signed a new contract to decorate the home of the mayor of Indian Hills. She's crazy hyped, not because the mayor is super rich, but because she knows she can make his home into a "resplendent showplace," she says. I like her confidence. I wonder how you get to be like that.

After a stop at AutoZone to get new windshield wipers for Darren's car (Darren is so proud of his red Ford Focus, not new, but safe, as Dad insisted, that he'll use any excuse to drive it, even if it's just to get me at school) we finally head to Dad's house.

Every time we pull up into that driveway, I still kinda gasp. The house is three stories, all brick, and it sits back from Indian Hill Road, deep, deep in a yard blanketed with that thick, bright grass you see in lawn care flyers. Its edges are decorated with tulips in the spring, roses in the summer, and mums in the fall. Anastasia likes to hire professional gardeners, but Dad planted the tulips himself. One by one. It's so pretty in the spring—they open up in the day, then close back up at night. And they come in, like, a zillion colors. I've got a dozen pics of those tulips on my phone.

The house has seven bedrooms, five bathrooms, three sitting rooms, and two kitchens. Yeah, two.

One near the downstairs recreation area—which, by the way, has a movie theater—and one for ordinary meals, I guess. Who needs all that? Me, I gotta admit.

Anastasia insists everyone remove their shoes when they come in. But to be honest—I love the feel of the Persian carpet on my bare feet. Since I'm confessing, I also love the view of the woods from the great-room window, the gleam of the hardwood floor in the family room, and the soft-peach colors of my bedroom. It's pretty awesome.

But most of all I love what Anastasia calls the music room. The walls are painted pale cream, the carpet is light blue, and sitting in the middle is a black Steinway baby grand piano. The keyboard is more than four feet long, while the rest of it stretches at least six feet. The lid is like a wing of a bird ready to fly, propped up to show the golden strings that create the sound. The piano, waxed and polished every week, gleams in the sunlight from the curved bay window. I swear that piano smiles at me.

The tufted leather bench beckons, and the keys sit ready for me to press on them. I never stop being amazed that these eighty-eight slices of ivory and ebony can combine to create harmonies. The keys way down on my left create thunder and booming and power.

And the keys off to my right can become morning and sunshine and tinkling laughter. It's just freakin' fierce. The music room is always the first place I go.

Now I sit up straighter than straight. I curve my hands, poise them for just a second above the keys, feel a swell inside my chest, then my fingers take over. I hit several chords and run a few scales. The perfect tones of the piano bounce around the room and back into me. I forget where I am and kinda disappear into my recital piece.

Anastasia slips into the room and sits quietly in the leather easy chair by the door. When I pause to pull out another sheet of music, she asks, "You don't mind that I sit here and listen, do you? I love hearing you play."

I can't help but smile. "No, it's okay. It's like I can sort of feel your senses suck it all in while you listen." I grimace. "Does that sound stupid?"

Anastasia smiles back. "Sounds exactly how I feel. Amazing how music can do that. When you play, it takes me back to when I was a little girl, when I was six, with two bows tied on the tips of my braids, and my grandmother was teaching me a few songs on *her* piano." Her face goes soft.

I've never thought about Anastasia as a kid. To me,

she's like a prewrapped package—already finished and perfect. And she played piano? How did I not know that?

"Did you take lessons too?" I ask.

She shakes her head. "Didn't have the money," she admits.

"Well, thanks for signing me up with Madame Rubenstein," I tell her. "She gets on my case, but I'm learning a lot."

Anastasia gets up and says, "May I?" before sitting beside me. Slowly at first, she starts picking out the notes to "Chopsticks." *Dup-dup-dup-dup-dup-dup. Plink-plink-plink-plink-plink-plink. Dup-dup-dup-dup-dup-dup. Plash!*

I can't help it. I do the same thing one octave higher. *Dup-dup-dup-dup-dup-dup. Plink-plink-plink-plink-plink-plink. Dup-dup-dup-dup-dup-dup. Plash!*

She plays her notes faster. So do I. Then even faster! Me too!

Pretty soon we are racing through the song, each of us using both hands, harder, faster, louder! My treble! Her bass! Then we play the whole thing again, double time, missing notes, ending with a giant crescendo, splattering the keys, and laughing like maniacs. "Whoa! That was fun!"

"I was going to enter your piano recital," she says, all fake serious, "but I decided it wouldn't be fair—I'd blow all you kids away with my mad skills!"

I crack up as she plays another few riffs—trilling treble to rumbling bass. Then she breaks into the beginning of a Chopin piece.

Wow. I had no idea Anastasia could play so well. How could I have missed that? And no lessons! It makes me feel a little intimidated—like, I wonder if she thinks that my playing is not quite up to par.

But she doesn't act like that at all. She gives me a hug, gets up from the bench, and stretches. "Now it's time for the real musician in the family to practice her recital piece," she says, then curls back into her chair to listen.

CHAPTER 15
Dad's Week

ANASTASIA OWNS A dog, a Maltese named Fifi. I do not like that dog. And she doesn't like me. But Anastasia loves the sneaky little beast, who has long white fur that flows around her like she's a little movie star. Her feet don't even show. She gets bathed and groomed every other week, with bows and ribbons and sometimes even toenail glitter. Yes, glitter.

Fifi likes to perch in Anastasia's lap while she works on her computer. She sometimes snuggles next to Darren while we watch movies on Netflix. She even lets Dad scratch her head and hold her.

But me? She snarls and shows her sharp, tiny

teeth whenever I try to pet her. I honestly think she's cute, and I would love to curl up with a real live pet instead of a stuffed giraffe, but Fifi wants nothing to do with me.

So today, after I practice piano, I decide I'm going to try to make friends with the dog. Anastasia keeps little doggy treats in the kitchen drawer. I grab a few and sit on the floor.

"Here, Fifi," I call in my sweetest voice. "Want a treat?"

The dog doesn't move.

"Come on, little pup," I say, trying really hard to sound sweet. "You gonna be nice this time?"

The dog simply stares.

I show her my outstretched hand. I move a little closer. Fifi doesn't budge.

I toss a treat across the floor. It lands at her feet. At first she ignores it. Then she sniffs it. Suddenly, in one swift movement, she gobbles it. She still has not budged from that spot.

I toss another treat, this time a little closer to me. Fifi tiptoes a few steps forward. Her bedazzled toenails click on the tiled kitchen floor. She grabs the second treat, then backs up, like I'm some kind of enemy. I leave the next treat right next to my leg. Fifi inches over, eats it, and—doesn't run away this time! I touch her gently. Wow, her fur is so soft.

I finally put out my hand, the last treat in my palm. Fifi sniffs it, grabs it, then runs into the other room. She clearly no longer has any use for me.

But I feel like I've achieved a victory.

CHAPTER 16
Dad's Week

SHOWERS AT DAD'S house are the best—he has one of those pounding, pulsing shower systems that spray water from the sides as well as the top, so the water smashes you everywhere. Sometimes I stay in that shower for half an hour if nobody notices.

Mom's shower runs out of hot water in fifteen minutes—gosh, she'd love this! I think back to how tired she's looked lately. This shower would wake her right up. But I think she'd still be sad—she tries not to let me see, but I know she cries every time we do the exchange thing.

I open up the bottle of raspberry soufflé shampoo and scrub *hard*. Mom says my hair lives in its own zip code. No matter what I do—mousse, gel, axle grease—it always looks like I just came in from a windstorm. My hair laughs at those cute hair products I see advertised on TV. Stupid, angry, springy fingers of frizz. It's a for-real mess. So I scrub and scrub. Soppy strands of my hair drip down and cling to my face. I try to let any thoughts of weekly custody confrontations—Mom and Dad practically snarled at each other today!— swirl down the drain with the sudsy water.

I pull a towel around myself quick when I get out because there's a huge mirror on the back of the bathroom door—I have no idea why. It's impossible to miss, and I don't like seeing myself naked. I'm a little too skinny—I can see the bones of my rib cage if I suck in my breath. It's odd to think I have a skeleton of bones hiding under my skin, holding me up.

"Naked" is an odd word. Just saying it makes me shy and embarrassed. I've seen pictures in magazines of models in teeny swimsuits. I could never do that! I pull my towel tighter, and even though I've showered, I lift an arm and sniff. I just smell like soap, but there have been days, especially after gym class, when, phew, the odor easing out has been kinda ripe. Anastasia bought me some flowery-smelling deodorant, so I roll that on, just in case.

I peer real close at my face in the mirror. Is that a zit? Nope. Another phew. I step back, and from about a foot away I see both my parents in my features.

I've got Mom's freckles and her fingers, which are long and limber and make it easy to reach across my keyboard. But I've got the thickness and curliness of Dad's dark hair. I've got Dad's fuzzy eyebrows. Mom's green eyes. Dad's wide nose. Mom's thin lips. Dad's oddly curled ears. Mom's long lashes. Dad's big-toothed smile. Mom's wide forehead. Dad's strong chin. Mom's bony legs. It's like half of Dad and half of Mom got put in a blender, and the churned-up result was me.

I squish out a big glob of body lotion—it's called Dazzling Dahlia. I have no idea if the actual dahlia flower smells this good, but this lotion is working just right for me today. I make sure my knees and elbows are slathered and as smooth as they're gonna be.

I wonder when the two moms in my life will let me wear makeup. Ha! On that subject I bet they both agree: *Let's make Isabella wait until she's really old—like twenty-one—before we allow her to wear lipstick or feel real pretty.*

Looking at myself right now in this mirror, I don't feel pretty at all—just clean.

CHAPTER 17
Mom's Week

IT'S FUNNY—WHEN Dad was in California, Mom's house was where I *lived*. It was *home*. But now I don't really feel like I have a home—it's more like I live at Dad's place. Or Mom's place. I never say "I'm going home" anymore. It's "I'm going to my mom's." Or "I'm going to my dad's." Going. Not staying. Actually, it's not funny at all.

The changing of the guard at the mall happened without a problem yesterday. At least for the grown-ups. I got there with Dad. I left with Mom. No fireworks. No ugly words. Just the exchange.

This morning I don't want to get out of bed—my

quilt is so warm. In a minute Mom will be in.

My room here is tiny, but I love it. I've got posters of my favorite singers on the wall, a small stack of books I want to read, several candles with cool names like Jasmine Morning and Mango Mist, and a large framed picture of a girl with her arms crossed and her face frowned up in anger, saying, "I'm still kinda mad they never told me how to get to Sesame Street!" That cracks me up.

The paint is chipping in several places, and I can see peeks of the pink the room used to be. It's now painted kind of a seafoam green.

For some reason, even though I never ever told her that, Mom thinks my favorite color is green. She goes out of her way to get me green water bottles, green pencils, or new green curtains for my windows. I've never had the nerve to tell her I actually like lavender better. She thinks green makes me happy, so I let her do her green thing. A couple of weeks ago she bought me a new T-shirt with that triangle/arrow recycle symbol. The slogan underneath says, "I recycle—I wore this shirt yesterday!" Of course it's green.

My room is a disaster right now. For *sure* I gotta clean this up after school! I've been making slime, and even though Mom hollers at me to put all that stuff away, it's kinda everywhere. I've got glue, Mom's baking soda, a four-pound box of borax, and several vials of food coloring. I keep my slime in teeny little Tupperware containers—the stacks keep getting bigger. I'm taking the lavender and orange ones to school tomorrow to show Imani and Heather. Imani told me she found a way to make shiny silver slime. I can't wait.

I keep the new calendar I got for Christmas on the wall right above my bed. It's marked off in weeks. I've colored the Mom weeks with green highlighter. And Dad weeks with neon orange. Twenty-six for each one. Split exactly in half.

Know what's sad? There are no weeks for me.

CHAPTER 18
Mom's Week

THEY'RE SCREAMING AT each other.

My mom and my dad.

Over the phone.

About me.

It's gotten worse since Dad moved back to Cincinnati—they're, like, territorial! Hey, I used a vocab word! I zap some ramen noodles in the microwave real quick so I can disappear into my room. Mom paces as she talks, flails her arms for emphasis as if Dad can see her, clenching her cell phone like it's a kitchen sponge after a messy spaghetti dinner.

I can make out only a little of his side of the

conversation, but I know exactly what he's saying.

Mom: "You think just because you come back to town, you can just swoop in and take over my child's life? Who do you think took care of her every need while you were jogging on some beach?"

I know Dad so well I can just about figure out what he's saying.

Dad (in that low, patient voice she hates): "I just want to take Isabella downtown to Music Hall this weekend to see the Cincinnati Symphony Orchestra. They are having a guest piano soloist from Paris. Rémi Geniet."

Mom: "Please don't do this, Isaiah, squeezing away my time with Izzy. I've got things planned!" Now she's circling around the kitchen table, brushing a crumb here, straightening an already straight chair. Round and round she goes. "You just can't change the rules to suit yourself!"

I will the microwave to cook faster—the water's not bubbling yet, but my stomach is. Every time they fight, I kinda wanna throw up. And they have no idea.

And Dad's now probably saying, "Please, Nicole. It's for Isabella's piano career." He loves to talk about my "career," whatever that means. It drives Mom bananas.

Mom: "Absolutely not, Isaiah! She's eleven. She doesn't have a 'career.' You get Izzy on Sunday as usual."

She knows Dad hates it when she calls me Izzy, so I'm sure he blasts back.

Dad: "I wish you'd stop calling her that horrible nickname."

Mom: "I don't care. I've got custody this weekend and we are going bowling. Me and Izzy. Izzy. Izzy!"

Mom taps her phone off, slams it on the counter, and starts sniff-snorting into a paper towel. She's trying not to cry in front of me.

"I love my new bowling shoes," I tell her as I scoot close. The microwave finally dings. "You think I can get three strikes in a row like I did last time?"

She pulls me closer. "You betcha," she says, kissing my forehead. I let her hold me ten, twenty, thirty seconds, then slowly I pull away. Mom is sensitive, so I have to be careful. I leave her in the kitchen and tiptoe to my room with the Styrofoam cup of noodles. No ramen at Dad's house—it ranks right up there with Kool-Aid to him. I shove my backpack off the chair so I can eat at my desk.

I'm the triple backpack kid. I've got my Mom bag—it's green, of course. Then I've got the lavender-print Vera Bradley Dad bag with matching lunch box, cell phone cover, and wallet. That's compliments of Anastasia.

And finally, I have a small black backpack with handles—that one is for my piano music.

I suppose it would make sense to combine the school bags, but like everything else in my life, I leave one at each house and switch which one I use every week. No biggie. I'm used to the hassle.

The only items that for sure go to both houses are my cell phone, my piano music, and my journal. My journal is black, ragged on the edges, and nearly filled up with my daily scribbles and screams. It's held together with a fat red rubber band.

But in both my Mom bag and my Dad bag I carry notebook paper and pencils, a phone charger, a wallet, a USB thumb drive, and my books. I gotta keep myself organized so I can keep up with Mom's world and Dad's as well.

Every single week.

Yep, I'm gonna be psychotic one day.

CHAPTER 19
Dad's Week

TUESDAY AND THURSDAY afternoons at Dad's house are piano lesson time. Madame Rubenstein comes from the music conservatory at the University of Cincinnati. Never to Mom's—my Casio is *not* what Madame Rubenstein wants me practicing on.

Her almost-white hair, so thin I can see her scalp, is always slicked into a bun. She never has a strand out of place. I wish she'd give me lessons in *that*!

She wears a different ring on each finger—even her thumbs—and about fifty gold bangle bracelets on her arms; they rattle as she plays. But her fingers are long and supple—she has no problem with pieces that are written for two octaves, no problem at all.

"Are you preparing for your recital, Isabella?" she asks in her thick German accent. She's fluent in French and Italian as well. "June ninth will be here before you know it."

"Yes, ma'am."

She narrows her eyes.

"I mean I'm almost ready—I practice every day," I assure her. "For more than an hour!" I add. I squint right back at her. She's got an attitude about my Casio. And she's never even heard it!

And sure enough, she asks, "But how many of those hours are spent on that . . . uh . . . toy?" She's trying to keep her nose from crinkling like she's smelling dog poop.

"My Casio works just fine," I tell her crisply. "My recital piece will be perfect."

But I frown as I begin, hitting the keys with anger instead of love, pounding, hard instead of light. *She's* taken the light out of the room.

Still, I practice chords and arpeggios, scales and phrases, until finally, she takes me deeply into the lesson for the day—a Mozart concerto this time. It's tough. Every note must be specific and clear, she tells me for the tenth time, so the sound "flows like water over the listener."

I press deliberately at the keys, head down, fingers connecting. The sounds are just not flowing today—anybody listening to me would probably think I'm gonna drown!

CHAPTER 20
Mom's Week

MR. KAZILLY STARTS history class with a question. "How many of you have been watching on TV or reading about the school protests happening around the country?"

Only a few kids raise their hands.

"I suppose we should spend some time one day figuring out the best phone apps for news and information for you all," the teacher says with a sigh. "But for now let's talk about how what's going on in other kids' lives can affect us all."

"What do you mean?" Logan asks.

"Let me explain," Mr. K. continues. "Do any of

you know *why* young people are protesting?"

Gretchen answers first. "Yeah. There have been a bunch of school shootings in the past few years. Students are saying, 'Enough of that,' and trying to figure out what they can do so it doesn't happen again. Maybe walking out of school can help change gun laws and stuff."

"It's gotta be crazy scary to have that happen at your school," Jontay adds, scrunching his face like he's thinking real hard.

Lots of us nod in agreement.

"Do students have a right to walk out of school?" Mr. Kazilly asks.

"Why not? They walked in!" Jontay says, breaking the tension a little.

"Do they have a right to protest?" Mr. Kazilly presses.

"Absolutely!" Imani says, her face serious. "Real people died in those school shootings—kids our age. We have a right to be safe."

"Very good, Imani," Mr. K. tells her. Then he asks, "What kinds of things in the past have led to demonstrations that have led to change?"

"Voting rights, uh, for women!" I offer.

"Racial discrimination."

"Violence."

"All of this is heavy stuff," Mr. Kazilly says. "In the fight for civil rights, for instance, there was sometimes violence. Terrible violence. But it eventually led to good as the minds and hearts of people were changed."

"Hmm. Not enough," Jontay mutters.

Mr. Kazilly then surprises me when he says, "Perhaps you're right, Jontay."

"I don't get what this has to do with us, though," Cecil says.

"Good point. Brings me around to what I planned for today. What I want to focus on are the many good books and stories that were written so that no one ever forgets all that happened. Writers rock!"

"Huh?" a couple of us say.

"And then *we* are going to write! This will be our sixth-grade start to making the world a better place," Mr. Kazilly finishes.

I think most of the kids in class either groan or sigh or roll their eyes, me included.

I raise my hand. "What are we supposed to write about?"

"First, you read and research . . ."

More groans.

". . . then you write."

Sighs.

Mr. Kazilly's taught sixth grade for a long time. He totally ignores our groans and pushes on. "Sometimes it takes a really bad thing to bring about positive change."

"Like what?" Jontay asks.

"Spent a lot of time reading your history homework last night, did ya?" Mr. Kazilly says, raising an eyebrow.

"The Celtics were in the playoffs, man! That was history in the making!" Jontay calls out. Lots of kids nod in agreement.

"Nice try," Mr. Kazilly says with a laugh. "Catch up tonight, okay? Chapter twenty-seven in your American history book talks about how churches were bombed, houses were burned, people were lynched. History— MADE." His face is dead serious now.

"What's 'lynched'?" I ask. I've heard the word before, but I'm not sure exactly what it means.

"Good question, Isabella. It's when people decide to be judge, jury, and executioner without following any laws. People were hanged or shot or imprisoned, without ever getting a proper hearing!"

"But . . . but . . ." I hardly know what to say. "That's really awful!" I finally exclaim.

Imani raises her hand. "Hanged? Like, a noose around their neck?"

Mr. Kazilly takes his time. The classroom goes quiet. "Yes. It was a terrible, terrible thing."

"They show that in cowboy movies all the time," Logan blurts out. "No big deal."

"I guess it would be a big deal if it was happening to you," Imani replies, her voice hard.

Logan puts his hands around his neck and fakes like he's choking.

"That is *not* funny, Logan!" Mr. Kazilly says, his voice rising. "Stop that!"

Heather looks squarely at him, shakes her head, and frowns. I'm not sure he notices—he's so busy acting up.

"Just doing a little show-and-tell." Logan does it again and pretends to gasp.

"I said STOP!" Mr. Kazilly actually yells!

"Okay, okay, my bad." Logan puts both hands in the air and tries to laugh it off.

Heather puts her head on her desk.

Imani, however, is standing up.

Mr. Kazilly finally notices her. "Imani?"

I've never seen Imani so angry. Her fists are clenched. Her face looks—how can I explain?—old, like a grown-up's. Like somebody who's lived a thousand years. It's kinda chilling. And impressive. I've never actually seen Imani really pissed off before.

She's staring Logan down like he's some kind of stranger, not the kid we've both known since first grade. "You, Logan, are an idiot!"

Everybody kinda sucks in their breath.

She narrows her eyes as Logan's go wide. "Real people were once executed by hanging. With a rope and noose. People like me! That is *not* funny. I'll say it again. *You* are an idiot!" And then she sits back down.

The room gets scary silent. Everybody stares at Logan, who's slumping as far down in his seat as he can without actually getting under it.

"Sorry," he mutters.

But he doesn't look sorry.

Mr. Kazilly looks from Imani to Logan and tells Logan he will see him after school for a whole hour of detention.

Logan starts to protest, but a stern look from Mr. K. shuts him down.

CHAPTER 21
Dad's Week

I LIKE GYM class most of the time. Grown-ups don't get how hard it is to be quiet all day. So screaming and hollering and bouncing balls is always fun. The only bad part is lots of us smell pretty funky afterward. The showers have been broken for as long as I've been at the school. Every year at the first-day assembly the principal promises that "funding will be available soon," but so far it hasn't happened.

The good thing is I have gym last period on Thursdays so I get to go home—well, whatever home I'm scheduled for—and shower. I gotta get the dirt of the day washed away.

After forty minutes of volleyball, we hurry back to the locker room to change and get our backpacks and stuff. Heather is sweaty and out of breath, all hyper because her final serve won the game for our side.

Imani had been on the other side of the net. "I coulda hit that!" she fronts.

"But you didn't, girlfriend!" Heather hoots. "Our side won!"

I get my backpack out of my locker and toss it onto my shoulders. Heather does the same. Imani is getting annoyed at her lock, which seems jammed. She gives it one hard tug and it finally opens. But then she stumbles backward, hand to her mouth, and lets out a scream.

I've seen a few scary movies, but I have never heard a real human let loose a real, honest-to-goodness scream.

We rush over—by this time she is kinda choke-sobbing. And pointing.

Inside her locker, dangling from the coat hook, is a thick rope, the kind we use in gym. It's knotted and tied round and round at the top. The bottom of it is looped. No—it can't be. No. But it is. It's a noose. A real, rope *noose*.

Having heard Imani's scream, other girls are surrounding us, looking shocked, everyone talking at once.

"What is that?"

"Where did it come from?"

"How could anyone *do* that?"

Cell phones are out. Photos are snapped—and shared, for sure. Teachers arrive. Imani, who at this point is sobbing, is led away. They won't let me or Heather go with her.

Chaos takes over. The police are called. Nobody is allowed to leave. This is crazy!

I didn't do anything wrong, but I'm so scared. One by one, every single student in our gym class is called into a little room.

I walk in and face the principal, the gym teacher, and a counselor. *What are they gonna do?* I want my mom.

This is what they ask me:

"What is your name?"

"Isabella Thornton."

"How old are you?"

"Uh, eleven."

"What grade are you in?"

"Sixth."

"What race do you put on your official school forms?"

"What? I'm not sure."

"Do you consider yourself Black?"

"I guess."

"Do you consider yourself white?"

"I don't know. I never really thought about it."

"Do you have friends of other races than your own?"

"Yes."

"Do you know any teachers who show racial bias?"

"No."

"Do you know any teachers who act negatively toward Imani?"

"No."

"Do you know any students who act negatively toward Imani?"

"No."

"Have you ever acted negatively toward Imani?"

"Huh? No! Of course not. She's one of my best friends!"

"How long have you attended this school?"

"Since fifth grade."

"What clubs are you in?"

"None, really."

"What websites do you follow?"

"I don't know. The usual ones. Just to do homework."

"Do you use Instagram?"

"Not very much."

"Have you ever been to a meeting about race relations?"

"What? No."

"Have you ever been to a Black pride meeting at your school?"

"No. I've never heard of anything like that."

"Have you ever been to a white pride meeting at your school?"

"No. I've never heard of anything like that, either."

"What time did you get to the gym today?"

"Just before class. About two, I guess."

"What did you do when you first got to the locker room?"

"You mean before class? I put my backpack in my locker."

"What did you touch in the locker room?"

"I don't know. A bench, maybe. The door. My lock. My locker. A wall. I don't know!"

"Did you leave the gym during class?"

"No."

"Are you sure?"

"Yes."

"Did you get back to the locker room before Imani?"

"I think we all got here about the same time."

"Were you ever alone in the locker room?"

"No."

"Where is your gym locker?"

"Number five forty-two."

"Do you know Imani?"

"Yes."

"Are you friends with Imani?"

"Yes."

"Do you know Imani's locker combination?"

"No."

"Do you know anyone who dislikes Imani?"

"No. She's nice. People like her."

"Do you dislike Imani?"

"Huh? No! I already told you—she's one of my best friends."

"Has Imani ever made you angry?"

"Uh, one time she ate my cookie at lunch. So I ate her chips."

"So there's been tension between the two of you."

"No. We're friends! We eat each other's food all the time."

"Have you ever had an argument with Imani?"

"No. Never."

"Have you ever seen Imani do anything suspicious?"

"No. Of course not."

"Do you know if Imani is associated with any racial pride groups?"

"Huh? I don't even know what that is."

By the time they're finished, I feel like throwing up. I don't see Imani anywhere. I found out later that her parents showed up really quickly. They were taken to another area.

They tell us our parents have been contacted. And school will be canceled tomorrow.

They finally let us go home.

CHAPTER 22
Dad's Week

NO SCHOOL TODAY.

Noose reports.
                News reports.
                        Police reports.
                                Gossip.
                                        Phone calls.
                                              E-mails.
Snapchat.
                Facebook.
                        Instagram.
                                Opinions.
                                      Anger.
                                          Confusion.
                                              Fear.

CHAPTER 23
Dad's Week

I WAS PRETTY much numb after being questioned. It was like something on TV! No smiles. Just crisp questions. But I can't even imagine what Imani had to go through. Somebody who lives in her neighborhood texted somebody else that police cars were in front of her house.

Dad and Anastasia really wanted to talk to me last night, but I just couldn't. . . . They were cool and let me just chill in bed for the evening. Even Darren knocked on my door, asking if I was okay, but he understood and left me alone. I fell asleep before dinner.

Now I'm up way early—even earlier than I would

be for school. I've been awake just thinking about . . . stuff. Writing in my journal and checking my phone. I'm usually psyched when we have a day off, especially when it falls on a Friday, but this feels so very wrong. I try to call and text Imani, but I guess her phone's off.

I wonder what Heather is doing, if she's okay, if she's as scared and confused as I am. I try to call her, but her phone goes right to voice mail too.

Mom has called and texted me, like, a million times. She's worried. I keep telling her I'm fine, but my stomach feels gurgly, and I woke up, like, a billion times last night.

Snapchat and Instagram are blowing up. Only a few of us were in the locker room, so it's *nuts* how people who weren't even there have so much to say.

Why a noose?
Why at school?
Maybe it's a sign.
Of what?
Bad things to come.
That makes no sense.
Folks are a little worried.
My uncle calls it "stirring the pot."
Your uncle doesn't even live here!

But why Imani?

I'm scared!

Of what?

Of what might happen.

I ain't scared of nothin'!

We should protest!

Protest what?

I'm ready to fight!

That's dumb—who you gonna beat up?

We oughta boycott the hardware store!

How do you know that's where it came from?

You need to go back to first grade!

Let's plan a walkout!

Why?

To get out of classes!

That's stupid.

You're already out, dummy!

But it would be fun!

Walkouts are serious things—don't play.

It's too cold to be walking out. Let's wait till next month.

I hear a gentle knock at my door. "You up? Can we come in, Isabella?" Dad asks, opening the door an inch, peeking.

I sit up. "Sure, Daddy. Come on in."

Anastasia's with him. She's wearing a silky-looking lavender top that's made like a sweatshirt. Dad's in a plain white T-shirt and pajama pants. He smells of fresh coffee as he leans over and kisses the top of my head.

"We just want to make sure you're okay," he says.

"Yeah. I'm okay. I guess. Maybe." I reach up to smooth my puffy hair.

"This whole . . ." Anastasia pauses, then says carefully, "This whole problem at your school . . . is very upsetting." Her forehead has wrinkled up.

"Do you want to talk about it?" Dad asks.

I look back and forth between them. I could say, *I'm fine*, and maybe they'd go away. But am I fine? No. I'm kinda freaked, so I go honest. "I guess I *am* a little scared." They side-eye each other and wait for me to continue.

"Because a noose means, well, a noose is what they used to hang people. Lynch people. Black people." There, I said it.

Dad sits on the edge of my bed as Anastasia says, "You're right. It's become a horrible symbol of hatred."

"But why *Imani*?" Just saying it out loud makes me angry.

"Well," Dad says, "it seems that her parents are

very active in a racial justice group here in town.
They drive people from underserved neighborhoods
to the polls so they can vote; they march in all the
women's rights and voters' rights and equal rights
demonstrations. They are the kind of people we all
should be—not scared to speak out and do stuff to
help folks."

"So somebody threatened Imani because her parents
do good things?"

"That's a possibility," he says, running his hand
along my headboard.

"Are . . . uh . . . you and Anastasia active in that
kind of stuff?" I ask nervously.

Dad does the finger-tapping thing he does when
he's getting uptight. "We donate quite a bit of money
to those causes. . . ." He stops.

Anastasia finishes for him. "But, honey, the truth
of the matter is we don't really *do* anything that folks
can see. Our contributions are behind the scenes."

Is it selfish I feel totally relieved by this answer? I
honestly don't care if they give a million dollars to equal
rights causes so the world can be better in the future.
Right now I'm worried about today. Sixth grade. The
only future I'm worried about is this coming Monday.
What if it happens again? What if next time someone

hurts Imani, like physically? Or someone else? Who looks like her. Who looks like . . .

I reach out and touch my father's hand. I look at my pale fingers next to his.

"Daddy?"

"What, sweetie?"

"Do you think people think I'm Black or white when they see me? Am I Black? Or white?"

His lips turn up into the slightest of smiles. I can't tell if it's a sad one, though. He looks at me with his bright brown-almost-black eyes, eyes with thick lashes just like mine.

"Yes" is his reply. "Yes."

CHAPTER 24
Mom's Week

MOM, OF COURSE, is still crazy concerned about the problems at school. She and Dad even had a brief conversation about it yesterday at the handoff, and there wasn't a hint of snarling.

She tiptoes into my room even before my alarm goes off on Monday morning. It's still dark outside. She lifts up Grandma's quilt and snuggles in next to me. Nothing is better than curling up with your mom first thing in the morning.

"You okay?" she whispers.

"Yeah. I am now." I snuggle closer.

"You can stay home if you don't feel safe, you know."

I pause. I know she'd let me if I asked. And I'm betting some kids will not show up today. But I actually want to go to school—I know, I know, that's just messed up! But I need to be with my friends. Imani still hasn't responded to any of my texts or e-mails. So I'm really hoping maybe she'll be there so I can see how she's doing.

"No, I want to go," I tell Mom emphatically. "I'm not gonna let one crazy person mess everything up."

"That's my brave Izzy!" she says.

"I'm not brave—I'm nosy!" I tell her. "The school must have figured out who did it by now. And I need to talk to my friends!"

"I'll see if I can rustle up a gourmet breakfast for us," she says, leaving her warm spot by my side.

"Can you pop open a pack of cinnamon rolls?"

"You got it!" she hollers as she heads to the kitchen. "And don't be dawdling in that shower like it's your own personal day spa, Izzy. You still have to make your bed and tidy up—what a mess in here!—and you gotta get to school on time."

I make a face, but say, "Okay, Mom."

In the kitchen, Mom, fabulous Mom, has made the cinnamon rolls. Her T-shirt this morning says, "I. Like. How. When. You. Read. This. The. Little.

Voice. In. Your. Head. Takes. Pauses." Ha.

Even though John Mark rarely drinks the stuff, he takes the time to brew coffee for Mom every morning. It's sitting on the table in her favorite mug, with three almond-flavored creamer packets beside it. John Mark is really nice to Mom that way. Between that and the cinnamon rolls, the kitchen smells extra good. It makes me feel like maybe the day will be okay.

Sweet rolls gobbled, milk gulped, jacket zipped, and it's time for me to go. Mom gives me a hug, and I lug my Casio, my backpack, and my piano music out to John Mark's truck, which he's already got running, warming it up. I sling my stuff onto the backseat, being careful with the keyboard. John Mark will bring it when he picks me up from school, so I can practice at Waffle House until Mom gets off work.

We are almost to school when he pulls the truck into a parking space about a block away.

"What's up?" I ask.

Finally he says, "This thing that happened at school, with your friend Imani, makes me sick to my stomach." Then he pauses. "And, well, I feel like I need to tell you a couple of things—about me."

I look at him kinda sideways. "Huh?" I'm wondering where he's going with this.

He rubs his hand across his face. Then he says, his voice low and quiet, "I know the kind of people who do horrible stuff like hang nooses."

Say wha . . . ? I wait one click, then ask him carefully, "You do?"

"Yeah, I grew up with them. My mom and dad— they were flat-out racists. I spent a lot of time hiding behind the sofa and bein' scared."

It's hard for me to imagine John Mark as a little boy. He's so big and tough looking now. "What were you hiding from?" I ask.

"My dad loved him some liquor, and he'd have his friends over every Saturday for whiskey and whatever. After they'd had two or three drinks . . . or more, they'd *really* relax and start talking smack. They'd say really nasty things about Jewish people and Black people and folks from other countries who lived here—basically, anybody who wasn't white." John Mark grips the steering wheel like he wants to snap it in half.

"What did you do?" I ask.

"Nothing," he admits, sounding sheepish. "Nothing at all. At least, not to my dad. He'd a beat the crap outta me. I was just plain scared of him."

I sorta understood.

"My father, he never changed," John Mark continues. "But I swore I wouldn't grow up to be like him. I ended up having friends of every color at school, and I knew that none of the stuff my dad said was true."

I look away. "I'm kinda glad I never met him."

John Mark's nodding, nodding. Then he turns to me and says, his voice suddenly loud for inside the cab of a truck, "I am NOT like my father, Isabella. You need to know that."

I look over at him. Tears have actually welled up in his eyes. *My mom has found herself a really good guy,* I think for the second time that day. And now it's me who's almost teary.

We sit in the truck in silence for a long time. Then he shifts into drive and we roll into the school parking lot. There are a lot more cars in the drop-off line than usual. It looks like kids who usually take the bus seem to be getting rides from their parents today. Then I count two . . . five . . . no, six police cars! Some have lights flashing. Some just sit there, in the way of the buses and cars. I lean forward. What's going on?

Kids are standing around, huddled in groups. Everything *looks* okay, but it just *feels* wrong. There are *police* everywhere! I'm starting to freak. What if more bad stuff happens? I've got a clencher grip on the door handle.

John Mark reaches over and squeezes my hand. "You've got this, Izzy. And I've got you. You hear?"

I blink. And breathe. I squeeze back. "Yeah," I say, letting my breath out in a whoosh. "I'm good. Thanks, John Mark." And I mean it.

Cars are inching to the drop-off point. John Mark stops the truck in front of a large group of Black students. They look like eighth graders.

"You sure?" John Mark asks.

"Yeah, I'm okay," I tell him. But I'm not okay. I totally have the jitters.

He seems to know this. So John Mark, the ruddy-faced, black-leather-jacket-wearing, muscle-bound, tattooed white guy, gets out, walks around the front of the truck, and opens the passenger door. He bows and offers me his hand. I take it and hop out of the cab. Then, with the truck still running, he walks with me right up to the front door of the school.

I'm too nervous to look to the right or the left. John Mark then winks, bows to me once more, and heads back to the truck, the heels of his boots thunking with every step. He climbs back into the cab and, purposely, I'm sure, revs the engine, just once.

Then, as the bell rings for us to go inside, someone touches my shoulder. It's Clint Hammond, the white boy with the gorgeous green eyes. What makes me reach up and smooth my hair?

"Nice truck," he says. Then he disappears into the crowd of kids.

CHAPTER 25
Mom's Week

TODAY MR. KAZILLY'S classroom is quiet, tense. Nobody jokes or goofs around. When the bell rings, we're all sitting, just waiting. Heather's in her seat, but no Imani. I bite my bottom lip. No Imani. Mr. Kazilly is wearing a sharply creased white shirt, a red velvet vest, and maroon slacks. He looks stupendous, to use one of his words.

"Sooo," he begins, "let's talk about what happened on Thursday."

I bug-eye Heather—he's really gonna go there!

Everyone looks down at the floor. He waits. And waits. Until I can't stand it, and I raise my hand.

"Yes, Isabella."

"I don't understand why anybody would do that," I admit.

Manuel raises his hand next. "It makes me afraid."

"Me too," Rochelle calls out from the other side of the room.

Mr. K. nods. "What do you think chases away fear?"

"A gun?" Heather offers.

Everybody whips around to look at her.

"No," Mr. K. says emphatically. "Guns only create more problems." Then he looks thoughtful and asks, "Is it possible the person who left the noose might be right?"

What did he just say?

Jontay half rises from his seat, scowling. "Huh? How you figure?"

The teacher continues. "In order to diffuse a bad situation, sometimes it is necessary to look at both sides of a problem."

"But . . . aren't they racists? The people who do stuff like this?" asks Otis, looking incredulous.

"I suppose we have to figure out the definition of 'racist' first," Mr. Kazilly says.

"It's somebody who hates Black people!" Otis shouts out.

"Yeah!" Jontay echoes.

"Hmm. Only Black people?" Mr. K. prompts.

Jontay's now standing all the way up. "All haters!"

The teacher pauses, then smiles. "You see what just happened?" he asks us. "In just a thirty-second discussion, look how easy it is to jump to anger and assumptions. Now let's take our time and dig a little deeper."

I watch anxiously. Talking about nooses and hatred and stuff is like swimming in the deep end of the pool. And I'm not a very good swimmer. Going by the look on other kids' faces, they aren't either.

Something clatters near my feet. Logan, who sits right next to me (Heather is totally jealous; her seat is all the way in the back) dropped his pencil. I reach over and pick it up, but as I hand it back to him, I see scribbles on a sheet of notebook paper on his desk, skulls and bones and guns all over it. His art is actually good—clearly he's got mad drawing skills. But his sketches are sorta, well, grim. He looks up, sees the look on *my* face, and smirks. I look away. He raises his hand.

Mr. K. runs a hand through his hair. "Yes, Logan."

"I kinda got a question. Since most bananas are yellow, what if a person doesn't like green bananas?

Does that make him or her a banana racist?"

"None of us are bananas," Rochelle argues. "This is about people."

She gives me courage to speak out, so I raise my hand. When the teacher nods my way, I blurt out, "I don't want to sound like a Hallmark card or anything, but I think the only thing that gets rid of hate is love."

Mr. Kazilly's nodding like crazy now. Nobody else in the class seems to be smiling, however. Kids are ticked off.

I'm starting to feel really stupid, like I've just said the cheesiest thing ever.

"Go ahead. Explain, Isabella," Mr. K. encourages.

I take a deep breath. "Well, it's easy to be mean. And hateful. I've heard . . . uh . . . my parents say horrible stuff to each other." I pause. It's like the whole class is breathing with me. "But it's harder to be nice. It's sometimes really, really hard. But I think we ought to figure out how to turn this around. So nobody else gets hurt." I close my eyes fast. I can't believe I told my personal mess to the whole class.

"That noose was a sign of hate!" Manuel finally says.

"Yeah, white people do that kind of stuff all the time!" Jontay shouts.

At this, Mr. Kazilly jumps in. Now *his* voice is loud. Even angry. I press back into my chair. "Now Jontay, we will *not* have that kind of discussion," he says. "We are working on solutions, not adding more to the problem."

Heather stands up. "Uh, I'm white. Imani is one of my best friends and she's Black. But I'm scared too. And . . . and . . ."

"Yes, Heather?" Mr. K. encourages her.

Heather takes a deep breath. "Okay, so this might sound weird, but I feel guilty, like . . . it's my fault, because it was probably somebody white who put the noose in her locker."

"For sure it was!" Jontay says, totally throwing attitude.

Heather sits down, covers her face, and begins to cry. I know I should go to her desk and comfort her, but I don't. I'm a wimp. If I spoke up right now, would I speak up for the white kids or the Black kids? Or both? Or neither? I honestly don't know. I scrunch down in my seat. I'm feeling, almost, ashamed of myself.

Kids around me start mumbling, grumbling.

"I can't believe they haven't caught who did it."

"I'm gonna watch my back!"

"They gonna get you."

I'm wondering who "they" are when, to my surprise, a soft-spoken white girl named Tiffany raises her hand. "Maybe we should think about signs of love instead," she says hesitantly.

Mr. Kazilly claps his hands. "Wonderful idea, Tiffany!" Then he asks the class, "How do you think we can make this happen?"

"What's the opposite of a noose?" Toby asks.

"A Valentine heart?" Tiffany offers, more confidently now.

Mr. Kazilly beams.

Logan groans. "That's so second grade!"

"Nah," says Tiffany. "I think we ought to plaster the school with hearts."

If Mr. Kazilly could be more into Tiffany's ideas, then gag me.

Nobody speaks for just a click, then everybody seems to jump in.

Heather lifts her head. Her face is splotchy. But she says, "You know, she just might be right! Every time anyone sees a heart, they'll remember what happened to Imani. That can't be bad."

And you know what? I agree.

Heather's eyes crinkle into a smile as she gives me a for-real good-friends look.

"We need to send a bunch of hearts to Imani, too!" another girl suggests.

"Can we do this in class today?" someone else asks.

"Instead of vocab?" a boy named Kevin says hopefully. Everybody laughs.

"Absolutely!"

Boy, does Mr. K. sound relieved!

CHAPTER 26
Dad's Week

IMANI IS BACK at school today! She texted me and Heather, so we waited for her outside on the front steps. When she stepped out of her mom's car, I saw her take a deep breath. A week is a long time. We ran over, like, full speed and hugged her. "We got your back, girl," Heather whispered in our little huddle. And I kept repeating, I guess to myself and to Imani as well, "We are stronger than the haters. We are stronger than the haters."

"Thanks, guys," she said. "You're the best."

I guess we looked kinda weird, all clasped together like that, but I did not care one little bit. When we let her go, her eyes were glistening. She didn't cry, though. She sniffed, stood tall, then turned and told her mom she was okay. I think her mom waited in the parking lot a long time. She was still there when I looked outside as the bell rang for first class.

All morning Imani sat in each class with her back straight, her eyes alert. She sorta reminded me of a deer—watchful, waiting to bound away at any moment.

At lunch, just before Imani plunks down next to us like she always does, Heather and I jump up and give her another giant hug. I can feel her relax as we hold her.

"You good?" I ask.

"Yep. All good," she tells us. "For now." I believe her. "What's the latest?" she asks.

Heather dives right in. "Well, it's like this—I think the company that makes Doritos is cutting down on the number of chips in each bag!"

"Say what?" Imani laughs at her silliness.

"I'm counting. Keeping a chart. I'm gonna report them to somebody!" Heather gobbles two chips.

"Well, you just messed up your count. You're eating your research!"

"Oops! Well, you may as well eat some too!"

Heather offers the bag to Imani, who takes it and gobbles a few herself.

That's probably just what Imani needed—a Dorito distraction. I think it worked! Imani seems more relaxed than she did this morning.

Hearts in every color under the sun are pasted everywhere—the cafeteria walls are covered. Tiffany and a couple of other girls are still at it, taping more on the far side of the lunchroom.

"How's your baby sister?" I ask, trying to tiptoe around anything serious.

"She's so sweet—like a little chocolate drop," Imani says, pulling out her phone to show us new photos. Then she says, looking around at all the decorations that we've put up, "The hearts are really nice. It's like the school vomited construction paper."

Heather and I almost fall out of our seats laughing. Then I look at her, worried that might hurt her feelings. But she's cracking up with us.

"Just trying to show the haters they won't win," I say carefully.

"Cool," she says as she sips on a juice box. "Really cool."

Several kids stop by our table and say nice things. Even a couple of eighth graders. I'm genuinely surprised.

"Hang in there, Imani," several kids say.

"We got your back, kid," others say with stern nods.

"Ignore stupid people."

Jontay, carrying a tray with only a salad and a bottle of water, pauses at our table.

"Just want you to know I'm here for you, Imani," he says. "Anything you need, just holler. You need somebody to walk you home?"

Heather jumps in. "Me and Imani ride the bus together. I'll look out for her."

Jontay gives a chin nod, then disappears into the crowded room.

When Tiffany finishes with the hearts on the wall, she comes over and brings Imani a container of slime—three red globs, shaped into hearts.

"Wow. Thanks," Imani says, her face brightening. I can tell she's not faking.

I'm sipping on a Mountain Dew, which all four of my parents say is unhealthy, by the way. I deliberately drink one every single day—just because I know they don't want me to. I finish it with a slurp and a burp. It's almost time to go.

I stand up to take my tray to the trash, but walking toward our table is Clint Hammond. I sit back down.

He's wearing a red Ohio State jersey. Pinned to it is a small lavender paper heart. He stops. I tell myself to stay chill. But he doesn't even glance my way. He reaches out his right hand to Imani. "Uh, I just want to say I got your back, Imani. Me and my friends. Not all white people are haters, ya know."

Imani blinks hard, then smiles. "Thank you," she says. "That means a lot."

She offers him her own hand. They touch. Four fingers of her slim brown hand grab four fingers of his surprisingly large pale hand. For just a second their palms brush. Their thumbs latch.

CHAPTER 27
Mom's Week

DURING THE WEEKS I stay with Mom, she goes to the grocery store to stock up on my favorite goodies, like Flamin' Hot Fritos, Kool-Aid, gummy bears, Cocoa Puffs, and Skittles. And broccoli. Yep, broccoli. For some reason, I like it—raw or cooked with butter. I think Mom caves on what she calls horrible junk food because I always eat my veggies—well, except for carrots. Whoever thought digging up a random orange root—then eating it—was a good idea? Certainly not me.

On the evenings she has to work, she gets off at eight so she can take me home and get me to bed at what she calls a "decent hour." She won't let me listen to music on my phone with earbuds while we're in the car together. She says it's rude. We're supposed to talk to each other. She usually starts.

"How are things at school these days, Izzy?" she asks me tonight. "All this racial turmoil has got to be upsetting."

"Yeah, I know," I say glumly. "Things are okay, I guess." I shrug.

She clicks on her turn signal and checks all her lanes—she's a *really* careful driver. When she's safely on Montgomery Road, she asks, "What's going on inside, kid? Talk to me."

I let her drive a few blocks before I figure out what to say. "I'm not sure," I tell her. "It's confusing." I hesitate. "I've got friends who are white. And friends who are Black. We've got kids at our school from all races—and most of the time we all kinda blend without thinking about it, like cookie dough. But this noose thing with Imani has really changed the recipe, at least for me."

Mom waits a tick, then asks, "How do you mean?"

"Because I *am* that dough, Mom! Am I the chocolate chip or the vanilla bean? I'm not really sure."

Mom chuckles. But for some reason that makes me mad.

"It's easy for *you* to laugh!" I tell her. "You're white! You have no idea what it's like to be me!"

Mom sucks her breath in.

"Isabella," she begins. She hardly ever calls me that. "You're right! I will never know what it is to be you, because you are your own unique, beautiful, talented self."

"I'm not even sure what that means," I grouse.

"You'll figure it out one of these days," Mom says with a confidence I'm not feeling. "You know, your father and I don't seem to agree on much, except for the most important thing—in spite of our problems, we both have always been so very proud of you. Because you are half of me and half of him—and all of both of us. We love you so—"

"That's not what I'm talking about," I interrupt, trying to find the words for something I've never really said out loud. "I love you, Mom, but I'm not white. I never will be, and . . . I don't want to be. Because the half of me that is Daddy is stronger."

She draws in another breath, sharper this time. Her hands have a death grip on the steering wheel.

I gnaw at my lip—she doesn't get it, I can tell, so I keep going. "On official school stuff like state tests, there are lots of little info boxes that we have to fill in. One of them asks what race you are. They've got choices like white, Black, Latino, Asian, American Indian, and other."

A pause. "Which box do you fill in?" Mom finally asks.

"Well, I don't answer 'other,' because that's like being nothing, like maybe I could be Martian or something. I'm not nothing. I am something. I am *somebody*." I hear the tinge of sass in my voice, but I don't care.

The look on her face is like nothing I've ever seen. I hope she's breathing!

"I'm Black, Mom. African American. That's what I put on my official school tests when they ask. I'm Black and I'm proud of that."

I hear her breathe out at last. "And I'm so very proud of you, Isabella. So very proud."

CHAPTER 28
Dad's Week

MR. KAZILLY, who looks like some kind of bee in his yellow-and-black vest today, is practically buzzing with excitement when I walk into his class after lunch. "For the next week or so, we are going to dig into some Black poetry!" he announces as soon as we are seated.

"'Bout time," Jontay grumbles.

I look around the classroom. I guess about half the kids in our class are Black. Tiffany raises her hand.

Mr. K. looks up. "Yes?"

"Uh, are we doing Black poetry because of what happened with Imani?"

Oh no she did not *go there!*

I think everybody in the room turns to look at Imani, who glares right back.

"We are following the school curriculum, Tiffany," Mr. K. replies curtly. "Now, may I continue?"

Rochelle kinda smirks at her friend Erin. But I saw it. So did Imani. We lock eyes for just a second. There is some sort of shift in the classroom—like a temperature drop on an autumn evening.

But Mr. Kazilly drones on with the lesson as if nothing happened, telling us all about this guy Langston Hughes—how he wrote poems and plays and stories, and how he'd started when he was still in high school! I bet he wrote stuff when he was in the sixth grade, too. Mr. K. tells us to find a poem by Mr. Hughes, then write a poem kinda like it.

I remember seeing a few pictures of writers in our literature book—mostly boring-looking white guys with beards. A few women. But come to think of it, I don't think *any* teacher has ever mentioned the race of a writer. Hmm—*I* think this assignment is gonna be kinda cool.

I raise my hand.

"Yes, Isabella?"

"Uh, are there other Black poets besides Mr. Hughes?"

"Oh, lots and lots," Mr. Kazilly tells me. "I wanted

to focus on Mr. Hughes first, but now I want each of you to find a poet you like, and we'll practice writing a little poetry."

"But isn't poetry *hard*?" Tiffany asks.

A few kids join in with "You got that right!"

Mr. K. straightens his vest. Then he asks the class, "Just glancing at the samples in our book, which takes up less space on the page? A poem or a story?"

"A poem!" Tiffany says, still frowning.

"Just a few words. And boom, it's done! That's easier, right?"

Tiffany scratches her head, then smiles. "I think that was a trick question, Mr. K."

"Relax. Think of musical notes. Then make those into words. That's poetry!"

That's the first time anybody's explained poems like that. I think I get it! Tiffany stops asking questions, so maybe she does too.

He breaks us into groups and gives us the rest of the class period to use our tablets and laptops to start our research. I could do this all day. Wow! Poetry is kinda like my music—it paints a picture in my head, only with words.

I click on the names and photos of the poets we find. Langston Hughes. Gwendolyn Brooks. Maya Angelou.

Some new guy named Jason Reynolds; he's got awesome dreads—cool! And this poet named Paul Laurence Dunbar, who lived in Dayton (just about an hour away from here)! Somehow that makes me feel proud.

Jontay raises his hand and says, "My cousin goes to Dunbar High School—in Dayton. He told me Dunbar was from Dayton, Ohio, and the school was named after this dude!"

Mr. Kazilly nods and says, "Your cousin is absolutely right!"

"That's kinda cool," Jontay mumbles. "Can I do my research on him?"

"Great idea," Mr. Kazilly says with a smile.

Tiffany chooses Rita Dove as her poet. Kirsten decides on Nikki Giovanni. "How come she's got an Italian name?" she asks.

We all give her the head tilt—like, *So what?*

Lauren settles on Gwendolyn Brooks. And Mr. K. says I can do more research on Mr. Langston Hughes.

Class time goes by so quickly: I'm still reading stuff when the bell rings.

It's actually fun reading Mr. Langston Hughes's poems. This dude wrote *bunches* of them. Then I find the perfect poem. At least for me. I read it, like, four times *in a row*! I can hardly believe what I'm reading.

And he wrote this almost a hundred years ago? *Man!*
It's so, like, real—like today, even.

Cross
by Langston Hughes
1926

My old man's a white old man
And my old mother's black.
If ever I cursed my white old man
I take my curses back.

If ever I cursed my black old mother
And wished she were in hell,
I'm sorry for that evil wish
And now I wish her well.

My old man died in a fine big house.
My ma died in a shack.
I wonder where I'm gonna die,
Being neither white nor black?

So this is the poem I'm going to turn in for my
project:

Criss Cross
by Isabella Thornton

I love my mom
I love my dad
I wish they loved each other

My dad is earth and warm and brown
My mom is sky so blue
She's clouds and sun
He's stars at night
They're always out of tune

I'm a flower in the yard
About to bloom and grow
I'm pink and green and red and gold
I'm not what they expect
I'll never be the same as them
That's something they should know.

After I turn it in, it occurs to me that the rhyme and the rhythm of my poem really, really suck. But maybe I'll try writing more. It *is* kind of like music.

CHAPTER 29
Dad's Week

THE SELECTION I'M doing for Pianopalooza is by an Italian composer named Muzio Clementi. His full name is Mutius Philippus Vincentius Franciscus Xaverius Clementi. Seriously. His mother actually named him that on purpose. I wonder if he ever got in trouble and his mom got mad at him and called him by his full name to come into the house. Probably not—he was a musical genius. Those kids probably never got yelled at.

Madame Rubenstein made me look up his history. I guess kids born back in 1752 in Italy had nothing else to do but learn piano and organ, so Clementi started when he was six. By the time he was thirteen, he had already composed lots of sonatas and symphonies. A couple of years later he had a job playing the organ at a church.

Overachiever, if you ask me.

I just want to learn to play this one piece he wrote and not embarrass myself. It's called Sonatina in C Major, op. 36, no. 1.

Madame Rubenstein grills me on the guts of the piece every time she shows up.

"What is the first movement, dear?"

By "movement," she's talking about sections of the piece. "It's called *Spiritoso*," I tell her with certainty.

"And what does that mean?"

I thought it would mean "spirited," but in Italian it means "humorous or playful." Like laughter, I guess. The tempo of the piece, when I do it right, is fast paced, and yeah, it does kinda remind me of somebody laughing. I told her so.

"Very good, Isabella. And the second movement is called?"

I'm ready for her.

"It's called *Andante*. It means 'slow or walking,' not skipping and jumping like the first movement, so . . ." I think for a minute. "I have to play it more thoughtfully."

"Excellent!"

I knew she'd like that. I actually found the definition from Google Translate one night when I was bored, but I'll never tell her!

"And the third movement?" she prompts.

"It's called *Vivace*. It means, like, 'bright or cheerful,' like the music is in a good mood, so the musician has got to feel that. I guess the audience will feel it too, if I do it right."

Her bangles tinkle cheerfully as she claps her hands.

"*Molto bene!*" she tells me in Italian. That means "very good." "Now let me hear your sonatina once more. The first movement, please."

After my lesson I walk Madame Rubenstein to the door, then go back to the piano room. I found out the piano bench doubles as a storage place for some cool stuff. A couple of weeks ago, under a pile of old sheet music and practice books, I found a yellowed book of boogie-woogie pieces, and old-time blues and rock. Awesome. I bet they were Anastasia's from a million years ago. Now I sit back down at the keys, flip to a song called "Bumble Boogie," and go at it. This is *so* not Clementi!

My fingers know exactly when to pound and exactly when to fly. I love the deep rumble of the bass and the syncopation of the treble. Yeah . . . *this* is the guts of music. Madame Rubenstein would have a heart attack if she heard me. I don't care. I don't even notice Darren at first. He's standing in the doorway, tapping his feet.

"Go, girl," he says. "Now this here is some real music!"

I stop, look up, and beam, out of breath.

"Yep! For sure!" I do one more bass riff—the fingers of my left hand dancing on the deeper-toned keys. "Is it good enough for ice cream?" I sing out.

"Absolutely!" he says. "Let me grab my car keys." I close the piano and yank a Windbreaker from the front closet.

"I hope they have strawberry chocolate marshmallow swirl—they were out of it last time," I tell him.

"Whatever you wish, m'lady," he says with a British accent. Then he bellows out, "Hey, Mom! Me and Izzy are going to get ice cream! You want anything?"

"Not this time," Anastasia yells back from her office upstairs. "You two have fun."

My mind is still pounding with the jazzy thunder of that piece. Makes me want to . . . boogie!

CHAPTER 30
Mom's Week

IT'S AN ORDINARY DAY.

Vocabulary words are projected onto the whiteboard.

Tennis shoes that used to be bright white are now dingy dirty.

Paper hearts on the walls have faded and fallen to the ground.

Pencils are stubs.

Pens are out of ink.

Several desks wobble as kids rock in their seats.

Three kids are wearing ear buds that Mr. Kazilly does not notice.

Imani sneaks out a York Peppermint Pattie. She'll nibble all the chocolate off from around the edges before the class is over.

Heather twirls her hair, up and down, through each finger, and up and down again. I doubt if she even knows that she does this.

I dig in my bag for my iPad.

And then it happens.

The principal, Mrs. Garcia; the sixth-grade counselor; and the school police resource officer stride into the room.

Mrs. Garcia announces, "Logan Lindquist—please gather your things. You need to come with us."

Say what?

I swivel around to see Logan grasp the edge of his desk, a look of panic on his face. He's gone completely pale. What did he *do?*

His eyes dart around the room, as if he's looking for a secret escape hatch.

I glance over at Heather. Her hands are pressed against her cheeks. I turn to Imani next—she seems frozen in place.

The school resources officer goes to Logan's seat and takes his arm. Logan closes his eyes, gives his head a quick shake, opens his eyes again, and then sort of stumbles to the front of the room. Without another word they turn him toward the door, march him out, and he is gone. I guess he forgot his backpack—it's still under his desk.

We sit stunned and silent.

Mr. Kazilly looks as confused as we do. After a breath, the principal seems to collect herself. She begins. "First of all, children . . ." (I hate that she calls us children—first and second graders maybe, but we're about to be in junior high—gee!) "I know this has been quite a shock. We had no way to shield you from witnessing that. I'm so very sorry. Now, I know you have questions."

Jontay already has his hand up. Now he waves it wildly. "What did he do—rob a bank?" A couple of kids cover their mouths to stifle laughs.

"No, of course not," Mrs. Garcia replies.

Jontay persists. "So what did they bust him for?"

Mrs. Garcia hesitates, then plunges in. "I'm really not at liberty to give details. All I can tell you right now is that we have *not* ignored the personal insult to Imani and the public insult to our school by the recent 'noose incident.' The investigation is ongoing."

She turns to Mr. Kazilly. "Continue with class, sir." And then she leaves. Does Mrs. Garcia really think we can focus on vocabulary after *that*?

CHAPTER 31
Mom's Week

I CAN'T BELIEVE Mom has given up one of her days to let me spend the night at Imani's house. I think she knows Imani could use a little friend time after everything that's happened. It's Friday, so there's no school tomorrow. Midnight movies! Yeah!

It took, like, a million phone calls and texts between Imani's parents and both sets of my parents to get this set up. According to some legal mucky-muck, both of my parents have to sign off on my staying with anyone else but one of them. There are permission forms and everything! What a pain!

Imani's mom picks us up after school. We sit on either

side of her baby sister in her car seat in their silver SUV.

"Hey, little Kendi," I coo. "I'm so glad you're awake. Oh look! She smiled at me!"

Imani strokes her sister's fingers, then, gently, the side of her face. Kendi's smile is like sunshine as she gazes at her big sister.

"It stinks that Heather couldn't come," I say as I dangle a fuzzy bunny in front of the baby.

"Yeah. Bummer. But I guess she couldn't miss her grandma's birthday party."

"We'll text her every five minutes!"

"Or at least every hour." Then she says, "Hey, Mom? Can we stop by the mall on the way home? We wanna hit the new slime store."

"Sure thing," her mother says, and puts on her blinker. "You girls want to hear some music?" she asks.

"Nah, that's okay, Mom. We'll just listen to stuff on our phones," Imani replies. "Your music is kinda old school!"

Her mother laughs, fakes like she's insulted, and says, "I'll show ya!" She turns the car radio up crazy loud to an oldies station, and we groove to that, singing all out all the way to the mall. I think the baby likes the music too. She coos and makes cute little baby noises as we sing.

Imani's mom lets us run into the mall alone to get our slime supplies—they've got new colors and fragrances and glitters, all kinds of different ingredients to use. I get stuff to make glittery gold. That'll up my slime game! We race back to the car, loaded up with fresh colors and possibilities.

Mrs. Bonner tosses Imani her phone. "Call the pizza place and order a couple. Tell them to deliver it. The order should get there about the same time we do."

"Thanks, Mom!" Imani says. We order one with double extra cheese and pepperoni, and one with everything except anchovies.

"What's an anchovy, anyway?" I ask.

Imani makes a face. "A totally unnecessary pizza accessory!"

The baby falls asleep as we ride. I show Imani a new game I found on my phone. By the time we get to level five, we're at her house.

It's funny. I've known Imani since third grade, but we hardly ever do sleepovers. I've been to a couple of her birthday parties, and she came to one that I had at the skating rink the year I turned eight. But everybody went to their own homes after it was over.

Imani's house is on a street that's like a half circle, so it's quiet with not much traffic. Her mom grabs the baby, car seat and all, and heads up the walkway. That thing has got to be heavy! Imani runs ahead of us and unlocks the door. Their golden retriever, Hash Brown, bounds out to greet us.

"Hey, Hashie!" Imani croons, trying to hug the dog, who runs in circles and yelps with joy. I think about Anastasia's little dog, Fifi, who rarely bothers to get up and greet anybody, especially not me.

We leave our shoes in the foyer, and I look around, finding myself wishing Anastasia could see this. The walls are painted in tones of orange and brown and gold. Paintings—all of them with images of places and people and animals of Africa—hang on every wall. Only a few of these were up when I was last here.

Masks. Framed mud cloth. Small sculptures. Beadwork. A tall wooden giraffe. Three small elephants—clearly a family—on a table. Two brightly painted but well-worn drums, the skin pulled tightly across the top, decorated with rope and beadwork.

"Wow!" is all I can say. I walk over to one of the drums. "Can I touch it?"

"Sure," Imani says. "My dad's only rule is always touch it with respect."

I run my finger across the top. So smooth. I tap it lightly with my three middle fingers. It talks back.

I quickly jerk my hand away. It gives me chills—the good kind.

"It's called a djembe," Imani explains. "You ought to hear my dad play it. He's teaching me."

We head upstairs to Imani's room. She's got twin beds—nice. Her room is painted pale yellow and also has lots of cool African decorations. A huge stuffed lion sits in a corner.

"The pizza's here!" her mom calls up to us, so we run back down and the kitchen is suddenly full of the rich smell of soft cheese and spicy sauce.

"Go ahead and take that stuff into the TV room, girls," Mrs. Bonner says. "Orange juice and Sprite are in the fridge. Help yourselves. I'm gonna feed the baby."

"Thanks, Mom," Imani calls as her mother heads upstairs. "We'll save you half of the pepperoni."

"You two clean up when you're done, you hear?"

"Okay, Mom! Got it."

Imani clicks on the big-screen TV, and we channel surf as we eat.

"I call the last piece of pepperoni!" Imani cries out.

"Not if I get to it first!" I counter, grabbing it. "Hey, try going to the movie section and let's see what we can watch for free."

"Good idea." Imani clicks on "Movies" and starts to scroll down.

"Nope."

"Saw that."

"Ick."

"My mom would kill us!" We laugh.

"Hmm, maybe."

She clicks again. And we both gasp. The selection is an old cowboy movie called *Hang 'Em High*. The frame shows a cowboy with a flat-brimmed hat, scowling like he's really angry. He's looking directly at a noose, which fills the screen.

Imani drops the remote and starts shaking. I snatch it up and click the red button to turn the whole system off. Imani won't stop shaking. I don't know what to do, so I call her mother. She must have sensed panic in my voice, because she comes running into the room. "What's wrong?" she asks, on full alert. She sits beside Imani. "What happened, honey?"

Imani's fighting back tears, still shaking like a leaf.

Mrs. Bonner looks at me. "What happened?"

"There was a . . . she saw a noose!" I stammer. "On the screen. It was from a movie. It just showed up really large on the big screen—we were just looking for something watch—and I think it freaked her out."

Her mother rocks Imani, back and forth, back and forth, until she calms down. "You okay, sweetie?" she asks. "Should I call Daddy to come home from work?"

Imani gulps and shakes her head. "I'm okay. Really. Don't bother Daddy." Then she looks at me, probably a little embarrassed.

I grab her hand. "Do you want me to go home?" I ask.

"No!" she cries. "Please stay! I need the company."

"Okay, but no more cowboy movies!" I tell her, handing her a tissue. Her mom nods in agreement and leaves us to ourselves. "Let's see if we can find *The Princess Bride*," I say. "True love and magical spells and all that."

"Bet," she says.

We actually find the movie and settle in to watch, both of us acting like nothing happened.

But later, when Imani puts it on pause so we can take a break to put popcorn in the microwave, I look at her. "You're still really spazzed out, aren't you?" I ask.

"Yeah. I get nightmares sometimes," she admits.

"I don't blame you," I tell her. "There was no reason for Logan to be so mean, and . . . hateful!"

Imani looks at me, her eyes pleading. "I just can't stop trying to figure it out," she says, haltingly. "But seriously, it makes no sense. I don't understand *why* Logan would do that! Like, just because of a class discussion, he had to make it *personal*? Like *totally* mean. I didn't deserve that!"

"True that!" I tell her emphatically. "Some people are just sick, I guess." I think back to what John Mark told me about when he was a kid.

"It just sucks. Was it because my skin is dark? I *love* my skin! I *love* how I stand out in a crowd of paler people! It makes me feel just really . . . really . . . proud!"

I look at Imani—what she just said blew me away! The sound of popcorn bursting is in the background.

"Can I ask you something, Izzy?"

"Sure."

She pauses, then asks, "Does this kind of stuff— you know, racial stuff—ever happen to you?"

I hesitate one click. Then I say, "Yeah. It does sometimes."

"Like . . . how?"

"Well, sometimes when I'm with my mom, people look at us twice. Like, they look me up and down, then Mom. Like, uh, *Are they* supposed *to be together?* Like a *Does she belong to that white lady?* look. You see what I'm sayin'?"

"Yeah. I get ya." She pauses, takes the popcorn out

of the microwave, and puts a dish of butter in to melt it. "What about when you're with your dad?"

"Nope, I never get those looks when I'm with him," I admit. "But on the rare occasions when I'm with my mom *and* my dad at the same time, like Sundays when we do custody exchanges, people sometimes *do* look twice, really quickly, to see why I'm with a white lady and a Black man."

I pour the melted butter on the popcorn. Then I ask, "What's it like to live with both your parents—at the same time?"

She shrugs. "Everybody's family is different," she replies, sidestepping the question. "I guess we just deal with what we got."

"Sometimes I wonder what it would be like if my parents got back together," I admit. "But that's not gonna happen. Not in a million years."

Imani nods thoughtfully. "That custody stuff must suck. I don't know what I'd do if I had to divide myself between my mom and my dad and move to a different house every week."

"It sucks scissors!" I tell her. "Now put the movie back on so we can focus on Buttercup and Westley and their search for 'true love.'"

We watch the movie twice before we head for bed.

CHAPTER 32
Dad's Week

TEENY HINTS OF spring are trying to sprout up already in Dad's yard. I guess it happens every year, but it always hits me how messed up the season is. One day it's freezing cold. The next day, like today, it might be warm enough to wear shorts.

I walk around in Dad's yard, checking on the early bird plants. The sun feels comfy warm on my arms. Tonight the temperature is supposed to drop down to the thirties. That's just plain crazy. Tomorrow, the weather folks say, it might snow. A couple of inches. I'm hoping for a snow day—woo-hoo—but I'm not holding my breath!

Dad's daffodils are almost three inches high right now. I can see the blossoms hiding under their greenish skin, waiting to burst out. *Wait a couple of weeks, guys, okay? Why are you up so early? You won't like the weather tomorrow.* I squat down and touch one of them, and I hear the patio door clunk behind me.

"You talkin' to the flowers again?" Darren asks, strolling over. He smells like he's fresh from the shower, wearing something that I call trying-to-smell-like-a-man cologne. I cough a little and smile to myself. He always wears too much.

"Yep. They're gonna get their little tushies frozen tonight."

"Spring flowers have been blooming too early for centuries," he tells me. "Every time a leftover freeze hits an overachiever bunch of flowers, humans panic. But the flowers just say, 'We got this. Chill.'"

I laugh. "Chill. That *does* sound very flowerlike."

Now Darren laughs. "Seriously, though, in a few weeks spring will be here for real, and those daffs will be sitting pretty, just like your dad likes."

"You always this smart?" I ask, squinting up.

"Only on Thursdays."

CHAPTER 33
Dad's Week

I ALWAYS VOLUNTEER to be a student guide on Open House night. It's fun to walk down the halls in the evening—everything seems to echo differently. The classrooms, which look perfectly normal in the daytime, look strangely odd when it's getting dark outside.

I've noticed that some kids have no parents come at all. But me, I get not one, not two, not three, but four grown-ups showing up. It's actually sorta comical. They have to pretend to like one another and get along. And they have to explain our family to teachers, who I guess have seen all kinds of unusual family situations. Watching the four parents in my life sharing the same crowded space is always a trip.

Everybody is aware of what happened with Imani, so it looks to me like Mrs. Garcia is working really hard to soften the uneasiness that's floating on the edges of everything. She's bustling around, chatting with families, wearing a grin that looks pasted on.

Every family is given a small brochure that talks about racism and how the community can work together to make things better. I really doubt a couple of paragraphs can change how people think or act, but I guess the school has to do something.

Lots of Hearts of Love are still plastered all over the walls. Classrooms display posters that say stuff like:

KEEP CALM AND LOVE EACH OTHER

HONOR OUR DIFFERENCES

TAKE A CHANCE—MAKE A FRIEND

ME—YOU—WE—THEM—US

ALL YOU NEED IS LOVE

HATE-FREE ZONE

I wave to Imani, who is walking to each class with her parents. They hover almost protectively on either side of her, stone faced. She nods at me, but I can tell she'd rather be anyplace else. She'll ditch them as soon as she can, I know, to help with guide duties. That's gotta be way less stressful.

I spend most of the evening directing lots of lost parents to their children's classrooms. Finally, one lady asks me to show her to Mr. Kazilly's room. I lead her up the steps, turn the corner, and there they are. Mom. Dad. John Mark. Anastasia. All four of them in the same room. Oh, man, I could play a piano concerto set to the uncomfortable looks on their faces.

Mom holds John Mark's hand.

Dad and Anastasia are, like, glued at the shoulder.

John Mark clears his throat several times. He has pulled a handkerchief from his pocket, and he wipes his face.

Anastasia's makeup is shiny—I can tell her face is sweaty.

When she's not clutching John Mark's hand, Mom's pulling her scrunchie on and off her hair. Twists it on. Pulls it off. Over and over.

Anastasia's hair, however, held like glue with hair

spray and gel, moves as one solid piece—almost like it's a hat perched on her head.

Dad's eyes dart from the windows to the doors to the ceiling, like an escape hatch might be up there.

And I stand at the door and laugh. They have to be nice to one another. *Polite* to one another. They are so pitiful it's hilarious. Weird—for once I'm the only one who feels relaxed!

I don't say anything to any of them—I just turn and leave. Let them suffer!

CHAPTER 34
Exchange Day

DAD AND ANASTASIA are late dropping me off at the mall. Over a half hour. It's unusual because Dad is usually so precise. We pull into the parking lot—it's packed. Anastasia's driving this time. She circles and circles. Dad's totally stressing.

"I'm sorry, Isabella," Anastasia says. "I just couldn't get away from my last clients. That was one talky woman! I bet I can tell you about every moment of the last ten years of her life!"

"Relax, honey." Dad keeps his voice soothing as he focuses on the parking situation.

"It's okay," I tell her. "Did they decide to let you decorate their house?"

"Yes! They put in a solid offer and gave me a deposit!"

"Well, then it was worth it," I reply. "But what's the big deal if we're late?"

Dad tries to explain. "Custody is a delicate dance, sweetie. Each side has to comply, or the judge can change the agreement."

I feel a little curdled in my stomach. "Like . . . how?"

"All I know," Dad says emphatically, "is that I'd like to have you every single day of every single week of every single year!" Then he hesitates. "But your mom would too. So I'm not messing up and risking the time I *do* have with you."

Anastasia swoops after a blue SUV that is pulling out and turns the car into the space—smooth. We scramble out and walk-run across the parking lot. The door in front of us is in the back of the mall, of course, the farthest away from the Apple Store. All of a sudden my father, like some kind of track star, shifts into a full-on run. I can't believe we're running—yes, running—my backpack thumping against my back.

We're sprinting past the Sprint store—ha, ha, no time to laugh at that—past Hollister, past Lush, bounding up the escalator, past Bose, a new Pink, and Alex and Ani, and down to the Apple Store.

Mom and John Mark are sitting there stiff as statues. Uh-oh. I can see Mom lifting her arm to check her watch. She glares at Dad. They stand as we arrive.

I turn and hug Dad good-bye. He's breathing hard. He embraces me, whispers how much he loves me, then I turn. I walk slowly to Mom and let her hug me. She, too, tells me how much she loves me.

I hear Dad walking away.

CHAPTER 35
Mom's Week

MR. KAZILLY'S WORDS this week are about bugs. It's all Heather's fault. She brought a dead caterpillar to class. She said she found it on the way to school and brought it in because the poor little thing looked just so sad. Weird, but yeah, I kinda agree. I felt sorry for it because it never had a chance to be a butterfly.

I never feel sorry for mosquitoes, though. I try to smack them before they land on my arm. But they get real sneaky and bite me on the back of my neck, or on the part of my arm that's hard to reach. Grown-ups tell me not to scratch, but the bites itch! I can't help it. It's amazing how something so tiny can bother me so bad.

Mr. Kazilly talked a lot about metamorphosis—how insects change from wormy-looking things to sometimes really cool-looking bugs. After bugs go through metamorphosis, they are called *imagoes*. Cool name. He said he likes to watch the sixth graders he teaches grow up to be teenagers and adults. It's hard for me to imagine myself as a grown-up, one of those imago things. Way too complicated to even think about.

The final word he gave us this week is "entomophagy." It means "the eating of insects." I'd have to be really, really hungry to eat bugs. If I were starving, I'd close my eyes, imagine that the bugs were chocolate-covered walnuts, then swallow real fast. And be glad I wasn't going to die of starvation.

I guess there really are some things worse than divorce and custody agreements. Like eating bugs for dinner.

Mr. Kazilly gave us a poem by some guy named Joyce Kilmer. What mother names her son Joyce? It's called "Trees." I guess Mr. K. chose it because bugs live in trees. I give up trying to figure out his motives.

Trees
by Joyce Kilmer

I think that I shall never see
A poem lovely as a tree.

A tree whose hungry mouth is prest
Against the earth's sweet flowing breast;

A tree that looks at God all day,
And lifts her leafy arms to pray;

A tree that may in Summer wear
A nest of robins in her hair;

Upon whose bosom snow has lain;
Who intimately lives with rain.

Poems are made by fools like me,
But only God can make a tree.

    I like the way he talks about trees having arms and hair and stuff. Mr. Kazilly has made us do enough poems that I'm not fooled by the tricks that poets play with words. But nobody actually mentions insects. I guess I have to figure that out myself. This is what I turned in.

Bugs

by Isabella Thornton

I think that I will never chew
A bug that's crunchy
  or maybe blue.
Bugs should buzz
  or crawl
  or fly
But never in my mouth . . .
  I'd die!

CHAPTER 36
Mom's Week

"GET UP, IZZY," Mom says, shaking my foot. "John Mark says if you hurry, he'll take you by Dunkin' Donuts before school."

That works. It feels like a hide-in-your-hoodie-'cause-it's-chilly kind of morning. I toss the covers back, hoping my Ohio State sweatshirt is clean. I find it in the bottom of my closet—only a little bit dirty—and slide it on.

Bed made—check. Face washed—check. Teeth brushed—check. Yesterday's jeans—check. Fuzzy boots—check. Hair smoothed—yeah, right!

I grab my book bag and head to the kitchen. I hear

John Mark's truck already running. Weird. It's too early for us to be leaving.

"I warmed it up for you, Izzy," he says, reading my mind. "If we hurry, we can beat the lines."

He must really want that Boston Kreme! I give Mom a hug good-bye and dash out into the chilly morning. John Mark seems agitated and distracted as he drives; he doesn't even turn on the radio. Doesn't even look for other big trucks. He rolls into the Dunkin' Donuts parking lot, then, oddly, pulls into a space instead of the drive-through. He leaves the motor running, revving it a little as he rubs his hands over his face, up and down, up and down.

"Uh . . . do you want me to go in and order?" I ask, a little mystified. "Are you . . . okay?" I've never seen him act like this before. He looks . . . scared.

John Mark takes a deep breath, then looks at me. "I'm fine, Izzy. Really," he says finally. "I just . . . wanted to talk to you alone for a few minutes."

When a grown-up says that, it's never a good thing. "Uh, why?"

His face is growing pinker by the second. I'm waiting for him to say more. I touch my phone in my hoodie pocket, just in case he's having a heart attack and I have to call 911.

"John Mark, you're kinda freaking me out," I whisper when he still doesn't say anything. "And I'm going to be late for school," I add, even though I know we're early.

He exhales loudly. "I'm sorry, Izzy. I just wanted to talk to you about your mom."

Now full-out danger bells ring in my head. "What's wrong with Mom? Is she sick? Is she *dying*?" I am instantly terrified. *Please don't let anything be wrong with my mom,* another part of my brain is praying crazily.

"No. No. No. I'm sorry, kiddo. I didn't mean to scare you. It's nothing like that. It's just . . . it's just . . ."

"What?" I practically scream. "What?"

He goes redder still, then blurts out, "I want to ask her to marry me. But I . . . well . . . wanted to ask you first. So that's what I'm doing—asking you. Would you be okay with that?" He gulps. "Do you think she'll say yes?" He ducks his head, almost like he's . . . shy! And he's asking *me* if it's okay?

"I'm messing this up." Now he's rubbing his face again. "Okay, okay, this is what I want to say: Would you allow me the honor of being your stepdad?" He's now so red I'm *sure* he's gonna have a heart attack!

But I'm also so relieved I almost wet my pants.

"Is that . . . it?" My really clever response. Not.

He jerks his head up and laughs. "I'm sorry. I've just never been this nervous before."

I open the door of the truck and hop out. "I'm going into Dunkin' Donuts, and I'm going to order a large coffee for you and a cinnamon bun for me. Get yourself together," I say, then stick my tongue out at him. "When I get back, we're gonna start planning a *wedding*!"

John Mark tosses me a twenty dollar bill. Wow! He really *is* feeling some kind of way today! His smile is kinda like Darren's when a girl he likes says she'll go to the game with him. All cheese.

I run into the shop, order an *extra*-large coffee, a Strawberry Frosted, and a blueberry muffin for him. For me, I pick out the biggest cinnamon bun in the case, plus an extra-large chocolate milk. I deserve it!

I stand by the door for a second, drinks and bags balanced carefully in my arms. A lady who is clearly in a hurry brushes past me, rushing to get out. I let her go by, because what John Mark just told me is slowly sinking in.

He wants to marry Mom. *He wants to marry my MOM!* This is gonna change everything. Or will it? I take a deep breath, then head out to the truck. John

Mark seems calmer, breathing almost normally, but he has not turned on the radio, so he's still a little freaked out.

We sip our drinks and munch on our pastries as if our minds weren't churning with unspoken questions.

When he downs the last of his coffee, he crushes the coffee cup with his hand, starts the truck with a roar, and backs out slowly. It's still very early, a full twenty minutes before we usually arrive at the school.

"You sure you're on board with this?" he asks as he pulls out of the parking lot.

I smile as brightly as I can. I lick the icing off my fingers and sip the last of my chocolate milk slowly. Ever so slowly. Then I tell him, "Yep. Go for it. She deserves a little happy in her life."

"I'm going to ask her real soon," he tells me. "At Waffle House. You think that's okay?" He's tapping his fingers on the steering wheel. I think he's terrified!

"Judy and Lucille and Mariah will love that!" I tell him. It's true—I know they'll get all crazy excited. It will be a day that Waffle House will never forget. Then it hits me—what about Mom? Will she want a marriage proposal inside a black-and-yellow-checkerboard-decorated diner?

And *then* what happens? My brain starts pinging

with questions. Will we move to a new house? Will we start doing everything together? The grocery store, the movies, as a threesome all the time?

And suddenly I have a vision of us as a new *family*. White mom. White dad. And me—the one who people take that quick second glance at when we sit together in a restaurant. As soon as Mom changes her name from Thornton to Metzker, I'm officially gonna be the outsider. Ughhhhh.

John Mark's fingers are finally relaxing on the steering wheel. I'm kinda thinking the steering wheel is glad about that. Bizarre, I know.

Well, good for him! I finally decide. He's still nervous—I can tell by how he's chattering about the weather, which is cloudy, and the traffic, which is light. He manages to get me to school on time—early, even. How can something so momentous happen and I still get to school on time?

CHAPTER 37
Exchange Day

THIS SUNDAY, it's Mom and I who are late for the Great Exchange. Real late. Mom's car is an ancient Chevy—built back in the nineties, I think. It would be cool if she fixed it up like an antique, but it's just plain old. And even though I remind her when I think about it, the car is way overdue for an oil change and a tune-up. The appointment slip, dated November of last year, is still stuck to the refrigerator door with a bumblebee magnet. So her car breaks down occasionally.

Today is one of those days. She's driving—John Mark's truck is in the shop. The car coughs, then farts, then just stops. She rolls it to the side of the street.

"Looks like we're gonna have a bit of an auto adventure!" she tells us.

John Mark gets out his phone. "I'll call Triple A. But it'll take them *forever* to show up."

Mom catches my eye with a gleam in hers and says with sass, "Don't worry—I got this!"

John Mark looks at her with a *Prove it!* face.

Mom smirks at him with the confidence of a lady who long ago figured out how to do things without a knight in shining armor to save her.

She pops the hood, fiddles with some wires, then pulls a toolbox from the trunk.

"C'mere," she says to me. She hands me a wrench. "Hold this secure while I turn this gauge."

I've seen her do stuff like this before—fix leaky pipes, unplug a clogged sink, or smack a glob of spackle on a hole in the wall. She tinkers with the guts of the car, getting her hands covered with oil. It takes her a while, but eventually she calls out to John Mark, "Crank it up!" He does. The motor gives one short cough, then roars back to life.

"You are amazing," John Mark hoots at Mom as she wipes her hands on a rag. He's looking at her like she's just cured cancer or something. She beams back at him. Oh, gag me.

"Are we gonna be late?" I ask, checking my phone.

"Not if I break the speed limit!" Mom answers, winking. She guns the engine and takes off.

But even though she hurries, and turns some corners way too fast, we are still crazy late as we pull into the parking lot. Mom's pale. John Mark's face is flushed. Even I am starting to sweat.

Then I spy Dad's Mercedes parked two cars over. Dad's sitting inside. This is not gonna be good. He must have gone into the mall and come back out. Ooh—not good at all.

Next to Dad's car is an empty handicapped spot. There are no other free spaces. Taking it is really bad, I know. So does Mom. But she pulls into it anyway. "We're only going to be a minute!" she assures us.

She shuts off the engine. I grab my bags.

Dad and Anastasia get out of the Mercedes and just stand there, arms crossed. They are not smiling, either, and they don't even have a *reason* to be upset after last time!

Mom and John Mark climb out of her car. No smiles there, either. I feel like I'm watching a bad TV movie and can't change the channel.

I scurry out of the backseat, my right shoulder braced against the weight of my bags, and kick the door shut. I honestly don't know what to do.

"Get back in the car, Izzy," Mom tells me. "Now. You don't need to witness this conversation."

She hardly ever speaks to me in that tone of voice. I hesitate, then open her car door. I put one foot in. . . .

Then Dad roars, "Isabella! Get in my car! It is *my* custody week!" His voice is downright scary.

I step out of Mom's car just as she hisses, "Don't you dare, Izzy! You get right back into my car!"

I just stand there, not sure whether I should turn right or left, go forward or backward, get in the black car or the tan one.

I sniff. I will not cry. I will not cry.

"It is *my* week!" Dad says, fire in his voice. "Isabella, move! Now!"

I'm standing in the middle of the mall parking lot, tears not listening to my not-cry order, rolling down my face. Folks are staring. And my parents are glaring at each other, not at me. I drop all my bags in a heap, then I plunk myself down on the asphalt.

"I'm not going anywhere!" I shout. "I'm moving to . . . to Paris! Why don't all of you just leave me alone!" I'm so angry I can't even cry. I sit there, arms crossed, waiting for the grown-ups in my life to come to their senses.

It's Anastasia who reacts first. Even though she's dressed in a velvet-looking business suit, she sits right down on the asphalt next to me and puts her arms around me.

Mom, of course, can't stand this, her ex-husband's girlfriend comforting me, so she runs over and sits down on my other side. Her soft apologies mingle with Anastasia's. Dad and John Mark just stand there, looking at the sky, at the cars, anywhere but at each other. If they say anything, I don't hear it.

Finally, my two moms—yep, I said it!—each take an arm, lift me up, and brush me off, and while Anastasia smooths my hair, Mom gathers my bags and places them carefully in the backseat of Dad's car. Then she walks back over to me and hugs me so tight I almost lose my breath. When she lets go, her eyes are filled with tears. She then does the unimaginable—she walks over to Anastasia, arms outstretched. The two women embrace.

I open the door to Dad's car.

Mom and John Mark drive away.

CHAPTER 38
Dad's Week

AFTER THAT MESS in the parking lot, Dad has been extra attentive, almost tiptoeing around me. I'm used to saying I'm sorry for doing stupid stuff—like for spilling nail polish on the bedspread, or for hiding a bad grade I got on a math quiz. But when parents apologize, it's just plain weird. Dad bought me a new pair of jeans, and he hates shopping in the teen stores. He keeps hovering when I'm practicing the piano, or saying good night, like, fifty times after I go to bed.

I just want the grown-ups in my life to act normal again—whatever that is. Is normal living week to week at different houses? Is normal never being sure of what normal really is?

I have no idea.

Since my slime stuff is at Mom's, I'm focusing on getting ready for the recital and practicing my music instead. I complain about Madame Rubenstein and her bangles and her snotty attitudes, but she really is a good piano teacher. My recital piece is nearing perfection, even according to her. But I'm starting to get nervous about the performance. What will I wear? How will I do my hair? What if my fingers get jumbled up?

As she left yesterday, Madame Rubenstein touched my shoulder and said, "You have real talent, my child. Treasure it." Then she took off one of the bangles and gave it to me.

"Thank you," I sputtered. "This is, like, awesome!" I was for real. The woman rarely gives compliments and seriously loves her bangles. I placed it on my wrist. It's way too big, but I love it.

"Don't feel obligated to wear it to the recital— it might slide down and make you miss a note!" she warned, but there was a hint of tease in her voice. "I just want you to have something special on your big day."

Now I give the bracelet a gentle twist. I think it's real gold. I'm gonna wear it the rest of the day. I play for another hour—serious pieces, and a fun little number that Anastasia found for me called "Choo-Choo Charlie."

Then I hear my phone ding—it's a group message from Imani and Heather, asking if I want to meet them at the mall on Saturday. Oh yeah!

We begin furiously texting as we try to figure out what to wear, what to eat, and what stores we will hit. Imani's mom will be there with us, but she'll just sit in the food court with baby Kendi. Her rule is that we just have to check in with her every half hour or so. Perfect.

We decide to wear leggings and long shirts, but not the same colors—that's for little kids—and Converse sneakers. I've got two gift cards left over from Christmas, one for Lush, so we'll go there. Heather—who is *so* lucky—got her ears pierced for Christmas, so we've got to hit Claire's for new earrings. Neither Dad nor Mom will let me get my ears pierced, but it's still fun helping Heather. Group effort!

Of course we have to hit that Pink store that just opened, too.

CHAPTER 39
Dad's Week

ON SATURDAY MORNING, I get out of bed and soak my hair in axle grease to make it lie down smoothly for the day. Well, not really, but I did find some extra-hold, superstrong hair gel at Walgreen's.

I'm dressed and ready by nine. I tiptoe down to the kitchen and make myself some toast. I'm very particular about my toast—at least at Dad's house. I like 100 percent whole grain wheat bread, thin sliced. I slather two slices with butter and pop them in the toaster oven for three minutes. They come out soft in the middle and crisp on the edges. That's when I layer on the jam—one with strawberry and one with grape.

Perfection! I pour a large glass of milk, and breakfast is fine and mine.

Darren comes in as I finish the last piece. "Izzy's famous toast and jelly," he says, pulling up a chair.

"Jam," I say with a fake British accent. "It's jam, sir!"

He cracks up. "Well, you've got jelly-jam all over your face, so here's a paper towel, m'lady!" He hands me one.

"What are you doing today?" I ask him when my face is presentable again. He's pouring milk over a huge bowl of Frosted Flakes.

"Looks like I'm driving you to the mall," he says. "Mom has a consultation at a house out in Milford, and your dad's playing golf." He stops and crunches. "Gotta love Saturdays!"

"Yep," I tell him as I lick jam from my finger. "I'm glad you're driving, though. We have to pick up Heather, and she'll freak when she sees you!"

He smirks, nods. "That's me—hero of the sixth grade!"

"I'll have to hold her hand in the backseat," I joke. "She will be having a heart attack. Can you come in with us?"

"Not this time—just have to make sure Imani's

mom is there, then I already promised the guys I'd shoot some hoops at the gym."

"Don't tell Heather," I warn him. "She'll give up shopping to go with you."

"To watch us play?"

"No, to play against you. She is *so* good."

"She's eleven!" Darren says with a flip of his hand, shoveling in more cereal.

"She's pretty amazing—she has four older brothers she plays with all the time. I wouldn't underestimate her!"

Darren laughs as I gather up our dishes and wash them, but I think about Heather and her brothers. I kinda like having a brotherlike dude in the house. Especially one who drives!

After Darren does the check-in with Imani's mom, and he heads out to the gym, it dawns on me: I have four full hours to just be me! Four hours of not belonging to anyone! It's not Mom's time or Dad's time. It's just a little me time. Is it terrible to admit I feel like dancing?

CHAPTER 40
Dad's Week

AFTER NUMEROUS WARNINGS and reminders, Imani's mom finally lets me, Imani, and Heather go off on our own. Slime store? No, save the best for last. We'll head to Lush first, we tell her.

"Have fun, little Lushies," Imani's mom calls after us as we jog off.

It smells good even before we get there. I think the Lush people must have a fan blowing scent into the mall concourse to make customers want to come in. Cotton-candy bubble bars. Ocean coconut. Mango mousse. Boysenberry lotion. Hyacinth bath bombs, and one called Cheer Up Buttercup. The place is like heaven.

"Whoa, I love her hair," I low-voice to Imani, nodding at a woman working there whose hair is streaked with purple and yellow and green.

"Ooh, look—Intergalactic!" Heather is squealing, holding a turquoise-colored bath bomb. It smells a little like peppermint. The purple-yellow-green-haired clerk tells us it spirals when you put it in bathwater, and kinda looks like a galaxy while you bathe. She looks as cool as the bath bomb. She's covered in ink— like dozens of tats—faces, flowers, birds. It's hard not to stare. Plus, she has more piercings than I can count. Even her name is cool—her tag says GRISELDA.

"I want to do that when I get to high school!" Heather says as Griselda moves to help another customer.

"The tats or the piercings?" I ask.

"Both," she gushes, still gawking.

"My mom would kill me!" Imani says wistfully. "But I feel so boring standing next to her."

"I feel ya," I agree. I look again at the lady's amazing hair. Then I think—if I dyed my hair purple, maybe no one would notice, or even care, how frizzy it is.

I tug on Heather's arm. "Ooh, look! It's Whoosh!" I laugh because it feels just like slime as I squeeze. We make our slime for less than a dollar. This stuff costs almost ten dollars, but then, it *is* professional.

The Lush ladies let us sample and sniff as long as we want. Heather buys the stuff to make mermaid water—a Big Blue bath bomb and a Sunnyside bubble bar. When you crumble it into the bathwater, Griselda tells us, it turns emerald green with gold shimmers. Cool!

Even though I usually take showers, I really want to try a Dragon's Egg bath bomb. It will burst into, like, a zillion colors but will leave a gold, shimmery center in the tub. I take it to the counter, dig in the little purse Mom got me last Christmas, and pull out my wallet.

"That will be seven dollars and eighty-eight cents," the salesgirl named Griselda tells me. I pull out my gift card and pass it to her.

Then she pauses, kinda tilts her head to one side, and says, "You are *so* pretty—really exotic looking!"

"Uh, thanks." I feel myself blushing. Exotic? What does *that* mean? Is that good? Or creepy?

Griselda's smiling, and continues, "Are you from one of the islands?" Before I can say I'm from six miles away from here, she finishes her question, "Or are you mixed?"

I open my mouth and close it, like a fish that's just

been pulled out of the ocean. This is not the first time someone has asked me a question like that. I'm never quite sure how to respond. This time I whisper, like I'm telling her a deep, dark secret, "I'm from the Isle of Patagonia—don't tell anyone!"

She nods like we just shared a joke. But it's *not* a joke. Now I wish I'd never come into this stupid store, even though I've decided she was complimenting me. Imani and Heather chatter about soap and lotion and head to the counter to pay for their stuff. I wait for them by the entrance.

Imani decided on a Marmalade jelly bomb—orange and yellow and smelling better than any jelly I know of. Their purchases are tucked into cute little bags, and she and Heather join me in a sort of floral cloud.

Heather makes me sniff inside her bag. "I'm never gonna be able to smell pizza again! My nose is full of honeysuckle!" I have to laugh, which helps bring my mood back up.

We pop in and out of a bunch of other stores, sometimes just to feel the fabric and check the prices. We hit a dress shop—way too expensive; a top shop—nothing cute there; then we find a place that sells only jeans. Skinny jeans. Cropped jeans. Even old-lady jeans that look like something out of a commercial for Rocky Mountain hiking. We try on seven pairs between us. Heather buys a pair with embroidered designs on the back pocket. Imani can't find anything that fits her height. The ones that are long enough are way too boxy.

"My mom special-orders lots of my clothes," she explains. "A girl's gotta do what she's gotta do."

We hurry down to check in with Imani's mother, then get slushies. I always order raspberry.

"Where next?" I ask as we drop one off for Imani's mom.

"Second floor!" Imani says.

"I'll meet you up there," Heather calls out. "Your mom says the baby needs a change, and I gotta make a pit stop anyway."

Imani kisses Kendi, we get warned again about all the stuff parents say to mess up a girl's fun, then Imani and I take off.

We head up the escalator and as we turn left toward Nordstrom, Imani notices a new store.

"Ooh, look!" she cries out, pointing. "It's called Prestige."

"Sounds expensive," I say.

"Looks like ladies' designer clothes," Imani says as we get closer.

Anastasia would love this, I think. I can already imagine her in that sleek outfit in the window.

We pause just outside the entrance, our purchases and slushies in hand. A security guard standing just inside the door gives us a once-over. I stare right back at him. He's blond, ruddy faced, and really built—the dude's got serious muscles.

"A *security* guard?" Imani whispers.

We're probably both thinking the same thing—what's so special about *this* store? We stroll past another couple of storefronts, then, as if we planned it, turn around together and head back to Prestige. We finish our drinks and toss them in the trash at the same time—*kerplunk*—and walk in. Even the air of the place smells luxurious. I recognize the Mozart symphony playing in the background. Why is it that people connect classical music to expensive stuff?

The security guard immediately leaves his post. I'm aware he's behind us, and I'm betting Imani is as well.

I let my fingers feel a baby-blue cashmere sweater. It's feathery light. I check the price tag—$495! I clear my throat and show Imani. She doesn't even touch it.

We walk quietly throughout the rest of the store. The purses are all by well-known designers.

A coral-colored leather one that I like is . . . $2,000. Whoa! I touch it with my pinkie finger. The leather is as soft as Kendi's face. The guard seems to edge closer. We are the only customers in the store.

We head to the back, where the dresses are hung on gold-colored hangers. Only one of each style is displayed. The man continues to follow us.

I lean in to tell Imani, "I guess they bring out your size," and as I do, the security guard leans in as well—almost like he's listening.

"I'm going to have to ask you to leave," he announces in a loud voice.

We freeze. What? Then I turn around. "Why?" I ask.

"Just following security protocol," he says. "This store is probably not the best choice for you two."

Imani gapes at him. "What does *that* mean?"

"This is a store for those who . . . can afford it," he replies, with a small, hard smile that really isn't a smile at all. "My job is to remove possible . . . threats."

"Threats?" I echo loudly.

A pale, slender clerk at the register looks up, then looks away in a blink.

"Yes. Now let's not make a scene. It's time to leave. I don't want to have to call the authorities."

"But we didn't DO anything!" Imani objects.

"Lower your voice, miss," the guard warns. "And please leave."

I'm not sure what to do.

Imani's face is scrunched so tight I can't see her eyes. I think she's about to cry.

I grab her right hand. She tightly clasps my left. With our brown fingers latched like a chain-link fence, we walk slowly, slowly—toward the door.

We pass by that cashmere sweater. Ever so quickly I reach out my right hand, grab a sleeve, and give it a swift tug. It falls to the floor like a wounded bird as we leave the store.

CHAPTER 41
Dad's Week

ONCE WE ARE well out of earshot, Imani is the first to speak. "So what was *that* all about?" she asks, her voice wobbly. "What did we even *do*?"

"Not one stinking thing," I tell her.

"Then why was he so mean? Do we look like criminals?"

"No, we don't. We look like kids. *Black* kids."

Imani's mouth falls open. She leans in, lowers her voice. "OMG!" Then she frowns.

That slushie is freezing in my stomach.

Imani breathes in and out, in and out, trying to get calm. Finally she says, "We are *so* not telling my mom," she announces. "Agreed?"

"Agreed," I say.

"I'm not sure she could handle one more incident."

I fix her a look. "Can you?" I ask.

She heads toward the escalator, then turns.

"Does it ever stop, Izzy?" she asks.

"Doesn't seem like it." Then I grab her hand and squeeze. "We will never, never step foot in that place again!" I declare, anger starting to replace the shock. "Even when we're twenty-five and can afford anything we want!"

Heather joins us at the bottom of the escalator. "What's up, guys? You look like you just licked dirt."

Imani and I look at each other briefly, nod, then tell Heather everything. She wants to protest, to picket, to write letters to the owners of the place.

"There's nothing to write," I try to explain to her. "How do you describe a feeling, a glance, a sniff, a roll of the eyes?"

Imani's face clouds over. "There just aren't any words. . . ."

"But . . . but . . ." Heather's eyes are tearing up. "Somebody's got to *do* something!"

But what? None of us have a solution. The three of us walk away, arms entwined.

We never did get to the new Pink store.

CHAPTER 42
Mom's Week

ON FRIDAY, AFTER John Mark picks me up from school, after the usual questions about homework and such, he announces, "I made a fresh batch of spaghetti—just for you!"

"It smells delicious! You know I love me some Waffle House food, but sometimes . . . homemade is the best."

"We'll head over to Waffle House in about an hour. Your mom gets off early."

"Yay! Maybe she can catch up on her shows tonight." I toss my stuff to the floor, wash my hands at the kitchen sink, and fill plates for us both, a double-large portion for him.

"I got ya, kid," he says, sprinkling tons of mozzarella on top of both of ours.

It is *so* yummy—spicy and full of onions.

"Wow, you're in a good mood," I tell him as I finish and he pulls a pint of mint chocolate chip ice cream out of the freezer.

He simply grins and serves me up a double portion. I'm for sure not complaining. As he sits down with a big bowl of it as well, he's humming and tapping out a beat with his spoon.

When I eat the last square of chocolate, he tells me I have a little time if I want to practice on my Casio before we have to leave.

"Let me help with the dishes first," I offer.

"No, no, you go practice," he says.

I *never* turn down a chance to play, so I quickly pull the Casio out of its case and set it up on the dining room table. I do a few scales, some basic review pieces, then jump full force into my sonatina recital piece. It's even sounding great on the portable!

John Mark, washing the million pots he used, hollers out, "Sounds great, Izzy. You're *really* good, kid!"

"Yeah, I know!" I holler back, happy sass. Then I turn on the drum and cha-cha beats, and I move into a jazzy, funky piece that I've been working on.

"Ooh! You are KILLING it!" he yells out. "Skills!"

"Yeah, I *know*!" I say again, cracking up, pounding some crazy bass notes to match the funky treble.

He dances into the room, clicking two handfuls of spoons and forks together like they're instruments.

"You're crazy!" I tell him as I finally bring it to a close. "But you dance pretty good for a white boy!"

Oooof! I slap my hand over my mouth. *Was that bad to say?*

But John Mark is grinning like I told him he won a million dollars. "Now, *that* is the best compliment I've heard in years."

I'm still rocking the keys, a little slower now, more mellow.

Then John Mark switches, goes a little serious. He pulls up a chair next to me. "I wanna ask you something."

I stop playing.

"Yeah?" I say. But I brace myself.

"I'm gonna do it tonight—the official proposal."

"Tonight?"

"Yep. At Waffle House. I want it to be a surprise, and I want to include you in this. You good with that?"

"I guess so," I say. Which about sums it up. I'm not *sure* how I feel, so I guess.

He takes a breath. "But before we go—let me show you my most recent ink." He nervously runs his fingers up and down the black keys. He stops, then rolls up the sleeve of his denim shirt. And whoa—there it is! Very small, on the inside of his left wrist, is my name, Isabella, penned in a really pretty cursive next to a small purple daisy.

I look more closely—wonder if it hurt to do that, and at the same time feel amazed—amazed that he'd do that for *me*.

"Wow! That's, uh, awesome!"

"You and me, kid," he says. "And your mom, who I'm crazy about." Then he adds, his voice a question mark, "If that's okay with you?" He looks at me with sorta fake puppy-dog eyes.

I can't help but laugh. "I've never been somebody's ink before!" I tell him. I honestly think what he did is really cool, but I'm not gonna tell him all that. At least not yet.

"This is forever stuff," he reminds me.

I get up and pour myself a tall glass of milk. I gotta give him credit. He's trying real hard.

○ ○ ○

"Hey, Izzy, I got an idea!" John Mark says, slapping his thigh as we drive toward the diner.

"What's that?"

"Let's go to Party City and get balloons!"

"Ooh! What a great idea!"

I look out at the sky—it's kind of a purple-rose color, with cottony puffs of clouds here and there, like a painting. Somehow that makes me feel like all this is gonna be okay.

At Party City the short, bearded guy who waits on us looks barely older than Darren. His name tag says HERBERT.

"How many?" he asks.

"About a gazillion! Every color in the rainbow!" John Mark tells him. "I'm getting engaged tonight, Herbert!"

Herbert laughs. "Gotcha, man!" He puts a small, limp piece of rubber on the nozzle. Then *whoosh*—it's a red balloon! And *whoosh*—the next one is green! And *whoosh*—it's purple! He ties each one and adds a string in one swift movement.

"I've always wanted to do this," John Mark tells me. He's almost as bouncy as the balloons. "I never had a birthday party with balloons when I was a kid—so these are for me, too!" I stay quiet and let him be eleven.

He lets me carry the balloon bouquet out of the store—it's huge! Stuffing them in the backseat of the cab is like herding birds, but I finally push them all in.

As we walk through the door of Waffle House, I can see Mom wiping off a table in the back. She looks beat. But then she spots us—me, John Mark, and all those balloons.

"Whaaaa . . . I've never *seen* so many balloons!" she says, delight in her voice. "But why? It's not my birthday. Ohhh, are these for Izzy? You are *so* sweet. . . ."

Now she looks confused. "But . . . it's not her birthday either."

John Mark hands me the balloons and digs into his pocket. He pulls out a small pink box. By now he's reached a whole new level of blushing—almost purple. He gets down on one knee. Mom gasps—sharply. Her hand claps over her mouth. Mariah gets out her iPhone. Arnie, the cook, does the same.

John Mark's eyes actually have tears in them! He opens the box. Wow! The ring is so pretty—it kinda glitters on the silky white satin.

"Nicole Theresa Thornton. I love you. I love Izzy. Will you marry me?"

It seems like all the air leaves the restaurant as

everyone near us inhales. At this point, customers are standing, peeking over.

Mom's chest is heaving—I can tell she's trying not to cry. Her smile, though, is *so* huge, so happy, that I feel a surge of happiness for her. But before she answers him, she turns to me. "Izzy, is this okay with you? I mean, this will kinda change our lives. I won't do this if you feel funky about it. I mean that."

Whoa. Whoa-whoa-whoa! John Mark's proposing to *her* and she's asking *me*? I don't hesitate. "Go for it, Mom. I want you to be happy." And I really mean it.

She reaches over and hugs me. "I love you, Izzy. You are my baby girl—now and always," she says into my ear. I squeeze my nose to stifle the sniffle I feel. I'm not gonna cry.

Now Mom turns to John Mark and says finally, "Oh, yes! Yes! Yes!"

Then he slips the ring on her finger. And they're hugging each other, and hugging me, hugging Lucille, and hugging Judy, and random customers are getting hugs—it's a flat-out hugfest.

I get so excited I let go of the balloons—about a zillion red, yellow, blue, purple, and green rubber globes bobble all over the ceiling.

Bobbling—exactly how I feel.

CHAPTER 43
Mom's Week

RANDOM THOUGHTS after the proposal:

Do I have to call him Dad?

Can he sign my permission slips for school?

Will I have to change my name?

If I do something wrong, can he punish me?

Will he make me eat carrots?

CHAPTER 44
Mom's Week

MORE RANDOM THOUGHTS—I've got a lot of them.

Well, I guess Mom and Dad will never be a Mr. and Mrs. again.

Truth: I gotta admit, I never stopped hoping, deep down, that they'd somehow get back together, you know? I bet most divorce kids do.

My mom is going to be Mrs. Metzker—instead of what I've always known her as: Mrs. Thornton. That's gonna be hard to swallow.

I guess *my* name won't change. I don't think they can make me if I don't want to do that. But I'm not sure.

I really hate the green paint on these walls.

CHAPTER 45
Exchange Day

ON SUNDAY THE mall exchange is practically pleasant. Mom and John Mark hold hands and actually smile at Dad and Anastasia as they pass the weekly torch in front of the Apple Store.

I'm not quite sure how to tell Dad that Mom is getting remarried. I imagine that would be her job, but I figure he might take it easier if I give him a heads-up.

I wonder if he'll be happy for her.

I wonder if he even cares.

But right now I'm focusing on the sweater Anastasia wants my opinion on. After we finished our Cheesecake Factory dinner, we wandered down to Nordstrom. Dad took Darren to Foot Locker—the newest Jordans are out—so we have time to browse.

The coral sweater looks beautiful on Anastasia, and I tell her so. As she's paying for it, I gasp. Off to the side is a black velvet dress—it has short cap sleeves, a rounded neckline decorated with tiny pearls, and a swirly, flowing skirt. I touch it and fall in love.

"Oh, Anastasia!" I murmur. "Look at this!" She turns to see what I'm talking about, then leaves the counter to join me. "It's just right for the piano recital!"

She runs her hands across the fabric. "Oh, yes. You're right. It's perfect. You'll look so pretty up there onstage. Run to the dressing room and try it on."

I do, and I gotta say, it rocks! Anastasia nods with approval as I flounce out to show her. She tells the clerk to add it to her bill, and I don't stop smiling all the way home.

CHAPTER 46
Dad's Week

FIFI IS WATCHING television when I get to my dad's after school on Wednesday. I'm serious. Anastasia leaves one of the television sets tuned to the Animal Channel when we all leave the house. She keeps the volume low—Fifi goes kinda nutty barking if an animal is injured and cries out in pain—but the insane little beast watches it like she's obsessed. Crazy, right?

My mother's been obsessing on TV too. I had no idea a channel exists that features nothing but weddings and bridal gowns and honeymoon possibilities. Twenty-four/seven. Seriously. I once got up to go to the bathroom at midnight, and I heard the theme music for *Say Yes to the Dress* coming from the living room. Wedding gown catalogs and ads for vacation locations arrive in the mailbox every day. How do all these places even know she's getting married?

Plus, it turns out that Mr. Kazilly's son is also getting hitched. What is this—a conspiracy? That's good news for him and his son, I guess. Bad news for us, because Mr. K. has decided to give us wedding words for vocabulary this week.

I'm really getting tired of Mr. Kazilly's passion for words. Is it possible for a kid's head to fill up and just shatter? It's enough I gotta do math and science homework, but this man seems clueless about other teachers or other stuff going on in kids' lives. Does he care that Heather has two basketball games this weekend? Or that Imani has the flu? Apparently not. Words rule.

The words this time are "bouquet," "misogamy," "boutonniere," "limousine," and "monogamy." I think he gave us "bouquet" because it's hard to spell. It's one of those crazy words that doesn't sound like it looks.

A boutonniere is a flower that a man wears in the button of his jacket. Darren looks good when he gets dressed up for a dance and wears a boutonniere.

He also gave us "fiancé" and "fiancée," two fancy

French words for the folks who are going to be married. The extra *e* on the end means it's the girl. (French kids must suffer as much as we do when they try to figure out their own grammar.)

Monogamy means "being married to only one person at a time." Makes sense to me.

Misogamy means "hatred of marriage." I guess that's how my parents felt before they split up.

CHAPTER 47
Dad's Week

I FINISH MY vocab homework in record time and head to the music room.

I like when I need the black keys—the flats and the sharps. They make the music jump out and grab whoever gets to listen.

I also like songs in minor keys—they're sad and deep and take me to a mountaintop someplace.

With the wind blowing.

And a child crying on a cliff.

And a wedding in a haunted castle.

And an eagle swooping close.

Yeah, that kind of messed-up piece.

When I play, I don't pay attention to the individual notes.

The notes become the melody. The melody becomes the rhythm. The rhythm is the harmony.

Whether I play the blues or boogies, concertos or cantatas, I forget about *me*.

I'm Bach. I'm Beethoven. I'm B.B. King.

And the *music* is me.

I'm a three-year-old in Italy, running though a field of daisies.

I'm a turquoise-backed African sunbird, soaring over the desert savanna.

The music slips out and shines like gold.

I'm a tiger running through the jungle, strong and powerful.

I'm a panther, dark and mysterious.

I am so strong.

I am in complete control of this world.

Chords. Arpeggios. Cadenzas.

Sharps and flats.

Major chords.

Minor scales.

Harmony.

CHAPTER 48
Dad's Week

IT'S STARTING TO feel like springtime—the weather is flat-out warm this April morning. Me and Imani are sitting on the front steps of the school, sharing a bag of grapes, waiting for the day to happen.

Heather gets out of her mom's car and joins us. She's sipping on a fruit smoothie. Plus, she's got a bag of Twizzlers! We make a space for her between us.

"So how are the wedding plans going?" she asks as she pops the bag of Twizzlers to share.

I crush the Ziploc bag of purple grapes until Imani gently takes it away from me.

Heather looks at me sideways. "Are you excited? Glad? Upset? Angry?"

"I don't know. All of that. I guess." I brush wandering strands of hair from my face. "My mom is stupid happy, and that's legit. It's her big day."

Imani, always practical, tells me, "Oh, c'mon, Izzy! Weddings are fun. You get to dress up and do fancy stuff."

I execute a perfect eye roll. "It's gonna be at the bowling alley! How fancy do you think it's gonna get?"

We all laugh.

"Well," Heather continues, "okay, so a bowling alley. That's . . . different. But you can still dress up; it's a wedding!"

"Yeah, I guess. At least they're not gonna wear bowling shoes and matching shirts. But it's going to take place on lane two—her lucky lane. Jeez!"

Heather: "The ceremony?"

Me: "Yep."

Imani: "Seriously?"

Me: "No joke."

Heather: "Who's invited?"

Me: "John Mark's family—I've met a few of his cousins, but there are piles of them coming in from

Michigan and Tennessee and California. He's never been married before."

Imani: "That should be fun. What about from your mom's side?"

Me: "More cousins. I'll be drowning in relatives I've barely met."

Heather: "Well, at least you'll have bowling to distract you in case they're boring."

Me: "Good point."

Imani: "You gonna have wedding cake and all that?"

Me: "On lane four."

Heather: "And flowers?"

Me: "Lane five."

Imani: "And a band?" We're all about to crack up.

Me: "Lane six."

Heather: "And food?"

Me: "Lane seven."

Imani: "And drinks?"

We yell it out at the same time: "Lane eight!"

By now Heather is laughing so hard that smoothie is coming out of her nose.

Imani: "And dancing?"

Me: "I don't know—in the parking lot, I guess." And now we're all cracking up. A couple of guys a few feet away are staring. I don't care.

"So have they set a date?"

"Saturday, August eleventh."

"That's only four months away!"

"No joke."

"Whose week is that?"

It's funny, or maybe just plain pitiful, that my friends know that *everything* I do depends on which week it is. "It's the Saturday of a Mom week."

My friends nod knowingly.

CHAPTER 49
Mom's Week

TODAY I GET out of the truck at exactly the same time as Imani gets out of her mother's SUV. She swings her clip-on ponytail and lopes toward me with a wave. She seems to be . . . relaxed! For the first time in ages.

At the same moment it seems like Clint Hammond is also meandering in my direction. I'm the tip of a shrinking triangle. I catch eyes with Imani. She notices, nods, and saunters over to another group of girls.

His hands stuffed into his jeans pockets, Clint stops just a few paces away from me and leans against the fence. He smells like cinnamon rolls. Maybe that's what he had for breakfast.

He's just a little taller than I am. I've honestly never seen anyone with eyes quite so green.

"'Sup," he says to the sky.

"Nothin' much," I manage to reply.

He says nothing for a couple of seconds. For the life of me, I cannot think of one single thing to say either.

"I think I saw you at Scatterpin Bowl last week," he finally tells me.

"Oh yeah?" I reply casually.

"I was with my dad. He's on a team, and they're thinking about moving there for their tournaments."

Hmm—this might end up being kinda interesting!

I look up at the sky and say, "Do you think they'll do it?"

"I think so, yeah. The bowling alley they've been using has gone out of business, and Scatterpin is closer for most of the folks on his team, so I guess yeah."

I kick the dirt a little, distracting him, I hope, in case my face is looking too excited. "You bowl too?"

"Oh yeah. I know how to blow a rack," he says, throwing a little pride. "I usually roll with the team on weekends."

I'm trying to ignore the voice in my head that's saying, *Well, look at you, all smooth and such.*

"My, uh, almost-stepdad is the manager," I explain.

"I hang out after school with him all the time. Maybe I'll see you around there."

"The dude with the awesome truck?"

I laugh. "Yep. He loves that truck more than I love banana cream cheesecake!" *So much for smooth!*

Then the bell rings and kids hurry toward the front entrance.

Without glancing back, he walks off into the crowd.

I almost trip on the front steps, trying to text Imani about what just happened. What *did* happen? I honestly don't know.

My armpits got sweaty. So that was weird.

I gotta ask mom to buy me better deodorant.

I know my hair was a mess.

Do I care if he noticed?

I shouldn't.

I don't.

It's *my* hair!

CHAPTER 50
Dad's Week

ON FRIDAY NIGHT Dad decides to take us all out to a place called the Capital Grille, near Rookwood Commons. It cracks me up how expensive restaurants, located in what are basically outdoor shopping plazas, give themselves these snooty, fancy names. Anyway, it sounds like a wear-a-dress restaurant, so I choose a yellow one—it's got a bit of sparkle to it. I don't think Mom has seen this one—I've never taken it to her house. *She'd like it,* I think as I twirl around in front of the mirror.

Then I smooth and resmooth my hair, pop a small bow on my ponytail, and squirt on a bit of jasmine-scented body spray.

When we walk inside, it's kinda dark, and soft music wafts from the ceiling. "Wafts" was one of our vocab words last week—it's like a movie-star word. Nobody real ever uses it. Except me. I think it sounds mysteriously cool. Fresh red tulips in crystal vases sit on white lace doilies on each table. Yep, kinda elegant.

Our waiter, who tells us his name is Cornelius, acts like we *are* movie stars or something. He keeps bowing, being . . . downright obsequious, like really kissing up to us. "Obsequious"—that was another word last week. I had no idea I'd *ever* get to use that one!

We don't go to ritzy places like this very often, so I order prosciutto-wrapped mozzarella as my appetizer, simply because I like the sound of the words. I pass on the soup and salad, and order Chilean sea bass. I like fish, even though it makes my breath stink.

I'm really hungry, so I'm glad when the food is delivered. Man, it was delicious. Like perfect. Like yummy. Like some of the best food I've ever tasted. Mr. K. would call it delectable.

"How'd your college interview go at school today, Darren?" Dad asks as he sips his red wine. "Yale. Nice. Was the interviewer impressed with your academic record?"

Dad is all about the creds.

With his mouth full of mac and cheese, Darren nods. "I talked to that guy for almost an hour," he tells us. "By the end of the interview he was sending me links for the best places to get food in town, and how to get student prices for the movies."

"Well, that sounds promising," Dad says, full of enthusiasm.

Anastasia is positively beaming. "I am so proud of you, Darren," she says. "Your father would be so happy."

"Yeah, I know, Mom. I'm gonna do this thing right. I'm actually thinking of going into medicine, be a doctor like Papa was." He cuts into his lamb chop.

I don't know much about Darren's father except he was a heart surgeon, and he was killed in a car accident when Darren was about my age.

Anastasia now turns to me. "So how is the recital piece coming? Feeling confident?"

"Yep, music's almost memorized!" I reply, probably louder than necessary. "Fingers ready."

It's the perfect time for Cornelius to bring the dessert menu. I notice they have cheesecake, but tonight I order something called Warm Double Chocolate Cake, which comes with cherries and ice cream. Darren orders the same. Dad and Anastasia both order raspberry tarts.

Darren's and my treats are delivered first.

"For you, miss," Cornelius says to me as he places the dish in front of me. "And for your brother."

At that, Darren and I exchange looks and then burst out laughing. Seconds later, we dive in. Best. Chocolate. Ever. I'm careful not to get any on my yellow dress.

When Dad's and Anastasia's desserts are ready, Cornelius brings them on a silver tray. Woven in a circle around the edge of the tray are long-stemmed strawberry-red roses. He bows as he sets the platter on the table, then backs away.

"Wow!" I exclaim. "Fancy!"

Then, seemingly from out of the shadows, a thin man in a tuxedo appears at our table. Crooked in his arm is a violin. He begins to play. I know this piece! It's Mendelssohn's Violin Concerto in E Minor! It's so pretty—like birds singing.

Anastasia looks confused but delighted. "This is lovely," she says to my dad. "Did *you* order the music for dessert, Isaiah? What a nice touch!" Then she gasps.

I see it at the same time she does—the blue velvet box in the center of the silver platter, right between the tarts.

She puts her hand to her mouth. She starts to cry.

Oh, man, here it comes! I did *not* see *this* coming! I squeeze my eyes shut. When I pop them back open, nothing has changed. Candle wax is dripping. Ice cream is melting. *And my father is getting ready to propose.*

I smile. In fact, I totally cheese it up. What else can I do? Darren is all teeth and grin. Dad stands up. He picks up the box and opens it. The light from the candles reflects on the diamond. Other diners seem to be looking in our direction.

"Anastasia Covington-McAdoo, I love you. I love your son. You love my daughter. Will you do me the honor of marrying me and making your name even longer by becoming Anastasia Covington-McAdoo-Thornton?"

The violinist continues to play. The ice cream on my plate continues to melt. Darren and I give each other a shrug and a high five.

Anastasia stands, brushes away her tears. "Oh, Isaiah," she croons. She squish-hugs Dad. She offers her hand to him. He carefully places the diamond ring on her finger. "Oh, yes! Yes! Yes!" she murmurs.

People around us are clapping.

The boring old men in the paintings that line the walls remain stiff and unsmiling—sorta how a part of me feels.

Does that make me an awful human being?

I think it does.

CHAPTER 51
Dad's Week

AS IF IT'S not messed up enough for my mother to be marrying some dude who is *not* my dad, now I have to swallow *another* stepparent. Well, I *do* actually like her. But still. There's gonna be four of them now!

Plus, now I have *two* weddings to deal with. This is insane. I'm going to have to find all those wedding words Mr. Kazilly gave us the other week.

I wonder how much a plane trip to Paris costs. I could ask for asylum. We studied it in school. It's when somebody who has no place to go or has big troubles asks a new country to accept them.

France has lots of musicians. I'm sure one of them will adopt me. If I show how well I can play, that might persuade someone. Piano teachers from all over Paris would be fighting over me! Maybe even Rémi Geniet. Oh, the music he could teach me! Yeah, him. I'd let him take me in.

The grown-ups in my family all seem to be going berserk with happiness. Mom is wound up like a fidget spinner. She bought a new dress—a purple, shimmery thing. She and John Mark went out to dinner; it was *not* a Waffle House! Ha, ha. He wore a gray suit and the new purple tie that Mom bought him. It matched her dress perfectly, of course.

Then there was Anastasia, chortling like a teenager when Dad had flowers delivered to the house—"Just because I love you," the card said. She keeps buying blank scrapbooks at the craft store. Three so far— embroidered and embossed and decorated with roses and such. Every speck of anything that might become a wedding memory, she tosses in there—stuff like jewelry designs and invitation ideas and flower arrangement choices and photos of gowns. It's like she wants to remember every single moment of the planning. And she's gonna need three more scrapbooks, at the rate she's planning!

Right now none of this actually includes me. I have nothing to do but show up.

And text my friends. We exchange messages late into the night. They are following it all like Mom keeps up with *Game of Thrones*.

CHAPTER 52
Mom's Week

AFTER SCHOOL TODAY, Mom says, "I've got a ton of clothes in my trunk that I want to drop off at Goodwill. I might even find a couple of surprises there as well!"

I like going there—it's more exciting than the stores at the mall. The clothes and jewelry and even the furniture all have histories, like they didn't just come from a factory—they had lives before they enter my life. I think that's kinda cool.

As we wander around the Goodwill drop-off center, Mom seems to be relaxed and in a great mood, so I guess this is as good a time as any to break the news to her about Dad.

"Uh, Mom," I begin.

"What, sweetie?" she responds.

"Well, you know how Dad's been dating Anastasia for a long time now?"

Mom nods. "He seems very happy."

"Yeah, well, that's good—'cause he's gonna get married again."

Her head swivels toward me. "Oh, really?"

"Yep."

She raises one eyebrow, just a smidge. "Are you okay with that?"

This conversation is just plain weird. Do normal kids discuss their father's wedding plans with their mother?

But I tell her, shrugging, "Yeah, it's cool with me . . . not like I had a say in the matter—ha, ha. But she's okay."

"Well, she seems to be very nice. I'm happy for him. And if you like her, then I know he's chosen well."

I thought . . . she'd be mad somehow. I honestly don't understand parents.

CHAPTER 53
Mom's Week

IF CLINT'S DAD decided to use our bowling alley, he didn't show up this week, is the thought that runs through my head as I roll through my favorite songs as well as my recital piece. I've set the record button this time, so I can hear myself play, find the blips I need to smooth out.

When I finish, I flop on my bed, pop in my earbuds, and push play. Who *is* that kid playing? Whoa! She's pretty good! Oops, a bungle. Gotta fix that. Ooh—perfection on that difficult part! Strokes to me! That performance is worth a couple of chocolate chip cookies! I head to the kitchen to claim my reward.

Mom's in there, phone to her ear, and she sounds livid.

Oh man. What now?

I pause at the doorway and hear, "You've got to be kidding me! What do you mean you can't change it? You canNOT get married on the same day that I am! I don't *care* about the cruise you've booked! There are *dozens* of those to choose from—pick one that's leaving on a different day!"

My first thought is *"Same day"? Why would he do that? And . . . on a Mom week!* Then my brain skitters to—*A cruise? This is the first I've heard about that!*

"I was trying to be nice by congratulating you on your upcoming marriage!" But her voice is far from nice—it's pure fury. "No, no Isaiah—it is not my problem that you didn't know the date. And I did not have to get YOUR permission to choose my wedding date, especially since it's during MY week." Now Mom's rubbing hard at my initials, which I'd carved into the table when I was little. "Look, I am getting married on Saturday, August eleventh. At eleven a.m.—The Chapel on the Hillside," she says.

Whoa! I'm really glad she decided not to get married at Scatterpin!

"And I've already hired a photographer, a florist,

and a caterer. I have put down deposits—*non-refundable* deposits. Case closed."

But I guess the case isn't closed because Dad's clearly saying something that makes her even angrier, if that's possible—Mom's about to rub clear through the table. And she's not havin' it—she hits him with her power play.

Her voice drops down low. I've never heard her sound quite so scary. "You listen to me, Isaiah Thornton. I hate that we have to split our child in half like the continental divide." *(Good one, Mom!)* "But come on—this is incredibly unfair to Izzy! Why would you do that to her? And if you insist that she attend *your* wedding on that same day, you need to set it for much later in the day, and you must make special arrangements with *me*. Because legally, it is *my* week! Is that clear, Mister Big-Time Lawyer?"

Dad says something and Mom replies, her voice lower and threatening. "No! Just no! Absolutely not; I am not changing my date. What about 'non-refundable' do you not understand? I don't *care* if August eleventh is Anastasia's birthday, or that her church is undergoing renovations, or that the heavens have prepared a rainbow just for the two of you on that day! Pick a wedding date that falls on *your* week. Figure it out."

I once saw a picture of a mother bear and her cub. The little bear was so small it could hide safely beneath its mom, which was roaring and showing her huge fangs at the approaching hunter. If that hunter had any sense, he hightailed it out of there in a hurry. That cub knew the fierceness and power of its mother. That's what Mom sounds like as she's talking to Dad. I am positive she's gonna win this round!

She stabs her phone off, circles the room a few times, then sinks onto the sofa and starts to cry—huge sobs. I watch her weep for a few seconds, unsure what to do, then I go over and sit next to her.

"Don't cry, Mom," I tell her, putting my arms around her. "Two weddings in one day! I can't wait—it's gonna be fantastic!"

This is such a lie.

CHAPTER 54
Exchange Day

THE WEATHER HAS been rainy icky all day. I can feel the tension as Mom and I head toward the Apple Store. We are late *again*. Insanely late. Like, two hours late. It's almost 6:00 p.m. Dad has texted me, like, four million times. I finally turned my phone off.

Today it's like Mom is out to win the annoy-Dad prize. It's like some kind of weird dance—like they purposely try to drive each other crazy.

This time Mom did it on purpose, and that's a fact. John Mark stayed home. Instead of heading straight to the mall like usual, Mom drove past it and made a sharp left turn into the Wal-Mart parking lot.

"What are we doing, Mom?" I asked.

"There's no better place to pick up wedding knickknacks than Wal-Mart," she said as she got out of the car. "They've got silk floral arrangements of yellow daisies—I *love* daisies!—I saw them online, and I've got to scoop them up before they're gone!"

"But what about Dad?"

"He can wait. This won't take long."

Good grief—this is gonna get ugly. She's so mad at Dad about the wedding business that it's making her whackadoodle.

She found the flowers she wanted, and some yellow satin ribbon and—so cute—small daisy-shaped candles. She then headed to the grocery section and started buying food! Corn. Beans. Chips. Cereal. Milk. Bread. Then, before we headed to the checkout, she said she was hungry and got us each a smoothie, then she headed leisurely to her car.

As we approach the usual gray leather exchange couch, I notice two other people standing beside my dad. I look over at the Apple Store—is there a new phone out? Hang on a minute—they're dressed in blue uniforms. With white hats . . . Police?

Why are . . . the police here? They all turn toward me and Mom. We get closer.

Dad lifts his chin—his *Don't mess with me* look. Anastasia is not with him. Neither is Darren.

What do the police want? My heart is thudding. I grab Mom's hand. She clenches mine.

One police officer strolls toward us, as if this is no big deal, yet his hand is on his holster. "Nicole Thornton!" he calls out. It's both a question and a demand.

"You called the *police*?" Mom hisses at Dad. "Because I'm late?"

"You refuse to follow the court order," Dad replies tersely, standing.

The policeman steps closer.

OMG! Are they going to arrest my mother? This is, like, crazy unreal. I gotta get out of here!

I let go of Mom's hand.

And that's when I can't stop myself. I run.

I take off down the concourse. I run full speed, faster than any laps I've ever done in gym, faster than when I got stung by a bee when I was six. I run.

I hear my name. Mom's voice. Dad's voice. They sound frantic. I can't stop.

I race down another concourse. My sneakers slap against the marble. It's Sunday, so most of the stores are closing early. I can't even run into one and hide. But I know this mall. Every inch of it.

The bathroom? No, too easy to spot me, unless I stand on a toilet seat like I've seen people do in movies.

I keep running. I'm gasping. Gulping. Sobbing. I hear Mom calling my name. Dad, too. He sounds kinda freaked out. I don't care.

I head to the entrance of Macy's, at the far end of the mall. A guard is closing the sliding glass doors. "Nooo!" I yell.

"Sorry, miss," the guard says. "We'll be back open at ten in the morning!"

I hear footsteps behind me.

"Izzy!"

"Isabella!"

I make a sharp left turn and spurt through the exit doors, into the parking lot. It's raining. Pouring. I'm soaked in seconds. I don't care. I bound into the grayness of the rainstorm.

There's really no hiding place in sight, so I press against the wall of the building, in the middle of a bed of freshly planted tulips and daffodils. I pull my jacket close—the storm is like liquid fury. Exactly how I feel.

My sneakers are sinking into the soft muck of the flower bed. The smell of fertilizer makes me gag. I just want to keep sinking into the mud until I disappear forever.

Mom and Dad come careening out the door. They spot me right away.

"Izzy!"

"Isabella!"

"I hate you! I hate you both!" I holler at them. I back away, wishing the wall would swallow me up.

"Izzy, come inside!" Mom is frantic. "Please! Come on, baby girl. You're gonna get sick!" She reaches out to me, but I retreat farther into the flower bed. She looks insane, her hair sopping, plastered to her face. She's crying too.

Now they're both slogging through the muddy flower bed. Inches away. I have no place to go. *Are the police gonna come out and get me now?* I'm scared. I can't see the doors.

Dad, his eyes pleading, his voice calm, says, "Isabella, please take my hand. Please."

But I don't. I bat it away.

"You called the *cops*?" I snarl. I wipe my nose with my arm.

"They're gone," he assures me. "Promise."

"Why would you do that? Why? Why would you do that to *me*?"

"I'm so sorry, Isabella. I made a mistake. A huge mistake." Dad sounds like he really means it. "Let's go inside and talk, okay?" His hand reaches out and touches mine. It is so warm.

I'm soaked and shivering. I'm so tired. Of. Everything. I let Dad take my hand. Mom brushes my face with her fingers.

They rush to embrace me. We are a sopping mess. The three of us.

But all I can think is that, for the first time in a long, long time, I am being hugged by my mother and my father at the same time.

CHAPTER 55
Dad's Week

DAD CAN'T STOP telling me how sorry he is. Grown-ups make mistakes, he says. Grown-ups can act stupid, he says. I don't even know what to do with his pleading words of apology. I don't want them.

I showered—stayed in there long enough to be pickled. When I got out, I felt fresher but not one bit better.

I threw my sneakers into the trash. Okay, so later I got them out again, but still.

Anastasia was so angry when she found out what Dad had done that she refused to speak to him. I know she would never have allowed the police to get involved if she'd been there.

She made me a grilled cheese sandwich, my favorite. I couldn't eat it.

Darren rushed home from a date. *He* didn't try to explain stuff away like Mom and Dad did.

When he walked into my room, I erupted into a full ugly-face cry. He sat close, handed me tissues, and didn't say a single word. Didn't even check his phone once.

CHAPTER 56
Dad's Week

ON TUESDAY, DAD knocks on my door.

"How's my Isabella?" he asks hopefully. He and Anastasia are still tiptoeing around me, but I am so over all his drama.

"I'm good, Dad. Why are you wearing a jacket? And what's up with the flashlights?"

He hands me one. "Grab a jacket, a hat maybe, and some gloves," he replies cryptically. "And wear your UGGS—the ground is wet."

"Huh?"

"Chop-chop. I've got something to show you."

"What? Outside?" But Dad's already headed down

the hallway. The weather has taken a nosedive, and all the tulips and irises that love the spring warmth are now probably huddling together, trying to keep warm. I'm not getting my UGGs all wet and gross, so I tug on my rain boots—the navy-blue ones with bright-white raindrops printed on them. I grab my winter bubble coat and a knit hat. I find my gloves already stuffed in the pocket, so I yank them on and catch up with my father.

He's already out the back door, the light from his flashlight a thin beam in the darkness. What the heck? I hurry after him—across the deck, down the steps, and into the backyard. His flashlight beam highlights a row of tulips—they are about to burst into bloom. They need just one more warm day, which *wasn't* today.

I walk-run, trying to keep up.

This is crazy! I think.

He's now at the far end of the lawn, stepping into the woods beyond. I've never been all the way back here, even in the daytime. What is he up to?

I smell something. I sniff. Something's burning? Wood, maybe? Maybe Dad is finally losing it. Then I see it—a flickering flame on the ground, a ring of stones around it. A campfire. Wow. Awesome. Why?

"What's up with this, Dad?"

"I decided to have a campout. For my girl. Just the two of us."

I gape at him. A campfire? *My* dad?

"I don't get it," is all I can say.

His laughter floats up and fades into the dark, starry sky. He offers me his hand, and we plop down on the folded-up blanket he's placed on the ground. He pulls me into a hug. "You know I love you, Isabella," he starts.

"Sure, Dad. I know." The air smells good—kinda old-fashioned and safe somehow.

"And I'm so very sorry about what happened Sunday. I hurt you. I embarrassed you. And I probably scared you to death."

I stare into the fire. "Yeah, all that and more," I say at last.

"We were really kinda dim not to consider how all our lives impact you and your life," he admits.

"True that."

"Anastasia had been trying to tell me that trying to get married on the same day as your mother was the wrong thing to do, but I wouldn't listen."

"Seems like she's pretty smart. You might want to stick with this lady," I say, elbowing him.

He pokes at the fire with a stick, then tosses it in. It flashes orange for a moment, then disappears into the flames. "I shouldn't have been so selfish . . . and . . . I didn't think about how our decisions would affect you. Dumb, I know."

I shrug. I like how the fire kinda dances and changes color. It never stays the same. Dad waits for me to say something.

Finally I say, "The thing is, nobody seems to ever think about how stuff feels to me. Nobody ever asks me—"

A log crackles and I jump. A huge spark bursts into the air, then—*spiff*—it's gone.

"I wish it could be different between your mom and me, Izzy."

I lift my head. "You haven't called me Izzy in forever!"

"You're my Izzy/Isabella," he says, sounding sorta emotional.

"Are you and Anastasia still coming to my recital?" I ask.

"Of course! We wouldn't miss it."

"It's just . . . Mom and John Mark are coming too. . . ." Now I pick up a stick and mess with the burning logs. "It would be kinda nice if the four of you could, you know, sit in the same room and listen to some pretty music for a couple of hours without—"

My dad can't interrupt me fast enough. "I promise. No more ugliness. Ever."

I'm thinking this might be a pinkie-swear kind of moment, but I let it pass; I'm outgrowing that baby stuff. Instead I just tell him, "I'm pretty good, you know," nudging his shoulder with my own.

"Of that I have no doubt—I've been listening to you play since forever!" He pauses, then adds, "It was your mom's idea, that first little toy piano. . . ."

Huh? I didn't know that. But I do know Dad is offering a major olive branch here, really trying to show me how bad he feels about Sunday.

It is so quiet out here—but then I realize it's really not. There's the crackling of the wood, the whooshing of the flames, the swishing of the new spring leaves in the trees above, a call of an owl, a rustling in the earth—maybe a chipmunk.

Dad breaks the silence by hitting me with a stunner. "Anastasia and I have changed our date, because it's just not fair to you. We're getting married the Saturday *after* your mom's wedding."

I chew on this news for a minute.

"I thought the church was gonna be closed for,

like, forever for fix-ups or something," I finally say.

"They are delaying the repairs for one week—just for us," he explains. "And for you, my Isabella. What we were doing to you was completely unfair."

"True that," I mumble for the second time. I'm not sure if he could hear my huge sigh of relief. We sit in the quiet darkness for a bit. The fire crackles and flickers, all red bright and dark-orange light. It never stays the same for even a second.

Finally I ask, "What made you decide to build a campfire? We've never done this before."

He chuckles. "When I was a kid, me and my best friend, Chango, used to build these every weekend. Since we lived in the country, it was pretty easy to just head out into the woods and set up camp. We'd pretend to be cowboys, eat potato chips, and talk smack. Then me and Chango would practice saying the dirtiest cusswords we could think of!"

This cracks me up.

"Fire made us feel like heroes. Made us feel stronger than we were."

"You ever do anything brave?"

"No, never did. Except maybe talk to you tonight," Dad admits.

"This is kinda nice," I let myself say.

"It's been a real long time since I had myself a campout," Dad says, poking at a log to stoke the flames, "so I decided to make me a fire and share it with my best girl. And maybe show you how sorry I am."

It's honestly hard to make my mouth say anything, but my stomach has no problem—it growls. "Did you bring marshmallows?" I ask, laughing.

"Right here!" he replies, victory in his voice. He reaches for a package wrapped in aluminum foil. "And hot dogs, too!" he exclaims. "But you gotta put them on a stick yourself—they taste better that way."

Just Dad and me. And the night. And the fire. And the smells of times long ago. We laugh. We talk. We stuff our faces. Just the two of us.

The hot dogs get burned, and the marshmallows melt, but this is the best campout I've ever been to.

Actually, it's the only one. But it was the best.

CHAPTER 57
Dad's Week

"YOU OKAY?" Heather asks at lunch today. I texted her and Imani last night to let them know I had a major update for them.

"Yeah, I'm good." I sculpt my mashed potatoes into a little mountain.

Imani narrows her eyes. "For real?"

I grab one of Heather's Doritos. "Not really, but what can I do?"

"So what did your folks decide?" Heather asks.

"First off, they agreed to be civil about arranging these weddings—no more fighting," I tell them.

Heather dips a french fry into her ranch dressing.

"You think they'll stick to that?"

"Yeah, I probably scared the poop out of them, going off the deep end like that."

They both laugh a little.

"So what's the plan?" Imani asks.

"You're not going to believe this, but Dad has changed his date!"

"Say whaaa . . . ?"

"Mom is getting married, as planned, on August eleventh. That's the last day of *her* week, her legal time, with me."

"And your father?" Heather asks.

"He and Anastasia decided to wait until August eighteenth. They'll leave for their cruise to the Bahamas the next morning."

"It's a miracle!" Imani cries out, lifting her hands up to the ceiling like one of those fake TV preachers.

"You're telling me! And all I had to do was spaz out and run a marathon through the mall!"

Just then, balancing a Styrofoam cup full of jiggling red Jell-O in his right hand and a cup full of wobbling green Jell-O in his left, Clint Hammond saunters to our table.

I pick up my juice box and sip fiercely, the box's sides going concave.

"Hey, I'm coming to the bowling alley with my dad on Saturday," he says easily, like we're best friends. "Maybe I'll see you there." Without another word, he pivots to his regular table, the gelatin still perfectly balanced.

"What just happened?" Heather mouths.

"Just some Jell-O," I manage to say.

We laugh so hard I'm snorting mashed potatoes.

CHAPTER 58
Mom's Week

MOM IS STILL going crazy with wedding stuff. She is obsessing over *scented* candles now—apparently the daisy candles are for "ambience" (vocab word—boom!) and scented candles are for "atmosphere" or something like that. Anyway, she's also dragged me to, like, a million stores to try on dresses. I had *no* idea there could be so many wedding stores in just one city.

Unlike Anastasia, Mom doesn't want long and flowing. "I'm looking for something knee length, with a full, flouncy skirt," she tells me, "so I can dance."

She finds the dress she wants at Marshalls. When

she tries it on, I swear she is glowing. It's a soft pink. It makes her face look like she's blushing. Which she is. Oh, gag me.

The dress we choose for me is a pale lime green— the only one like it in the store. Okay, so it's green. And ordinarily I hate green. But this dress . . . it shimmers with silver accents when I move. It makes me feel . . . pretty, I guess.

But if I decide to bowl, I'm changing my clothes!

As for John Mark, he's been waxing the truck every other day, making sure it sparkles inside and out when Mom has to ride in it. And he's redoing the bathroom and has changed the ugly brown tiles to a nice baby blue. He installed a new toilet seat. It's heated! Now, that's fresh! I can't wait to invite Heather and Imani for a sleepover—just so they can try our new toilet!

Tuesday night, exhausted from the flurry of planning and painting and plumbing going on (which I helped with, thank you very much), I pull out my Casio, place it on the kitchen table, and let myself go. Nobody seems to remember that I have a piano recital the second weekend of June. My sonatina needs work, so I play it again and again, going over the tricky left-hand fingering of that one tough passage a zillion times. When I master it, I'm feeling kinda proud of myself.

I also realize that while I was playing, not even once did I think about weddings. Not once—in, like, an hour! Woop, woop!

CHAPTER 59
Dad's Week

ANASTASIA IS ALSO in full wedding mode—of course! She has swatches of colors and samples of flowers. She has lists of menus and musicians. I gotta admit, though, Anastasia is doing her best to include me. I really appreciate it, but I don't know how to tell her. Like, what am I supposed to say? *Gee, thanks, my almost-stepmom. Even though nobody ever asked me if I even wanted a stepmother.*

Every day after school this week, Anastasia and I have gone out to investigate "possibilities," as she calls them. We listened to a band and an orchestra. We tasted cakes at four different bakeries. Okay, that part was fine by me—that lemon-filled cake was the bomb! We visited several photographers.

Today we are shopping for dresses. Anastasia is positively giddy. She fills every single dress in all the right places. I don't even have those places yet. And I don't see any dress that'll look good on me.

Maybe I can wear the same dress to both weddings—I won't even have to change! But then Anastasia pulls up at our final stop (number six) and says, "There's something in this bridal shop I want you to see. I have it on hold."

"Okay," I say, not really caring. I'm getting hungry. I could go for a Big Mac.

A saleswoman, who was a middle-aged Black woman, greets us, then hurries to the back when Anastasia gives her a green numbered ticket. The woman returns carrying a long, satiny garment bag on a wooden hanger.

I sit, done with dresses already, in front of a huge mirror and try to smooth strands of flyaway hair while Anastasia tries on her dress. She emerges from the dressing room minutes later and strikes a pose. "What do you think, Isabella?" she asks, her eyes hopeful. The dress is a pale champagne color, a full-length blend of silk and lace. I can't believe how good she looks.

I break into a grin. "That's the one," I tell her. "You look pretty fabulous." I mean it.

"Are you sure?" she asks, looking at herself from the back.

"Yep!" I say. "Dad's gonna melt when he sees you walking down the aisle in that."

"I hoped you'd say that," she tells me, almost shyly. Then she nods to the saleslady, who disappears back into the dressing room. She returns a moment later with a size-me version of that very same dress, only in coral. It's . . . gorgeous. I have never owned such a pretty dress.

"It's the mother-daughter dress," the saleswoman explains to me. "The trend is for the two most important women in the ceremony to dress alike. What do you think?"

"Mother-daughter?" I echo. I look at Anastasia. I like her a lot. She's really cool. But I have a mother. I have a sudden urge to run again, out of that shop, down the sidewalk.

Anastasia sees my hesitation, and she quickly interrupts. "If you'd rather pick out something else, there are lots of lovely bridesmaid dresses to choose from. I didn't mean to make you feel uncomfortable— it just looked like it would be gorgeous on you. . . ." The saleslady hurries away.

Well, it does make me feel kinda icky. But I don't

say that. I just have to think about it for a minute.

I stand there, staring at the dress.

"I've never had a little girl," Anastasia says, her bottom lip starting to quiver. But she takes a breath and continues. "I'd be honored if you would be my daughter for this wedding. My daughter, and my maid of honor."

I reach out and touch the dress.

"Let me go try this on," I finally say. She sinks into one of the soft leather chairs provided for people who have to sit and approve of others who are trying on clothes.

I have to admit, I look good in the dress. Really good. I smile at the mirror. It fits me perfectly. I walk out and twirl just like Anastasia did in front of the full-length mirror. The pale coral is soft and delicate—I feel like a supermodel or something.

The saleslady, back again, claps and cheers. "You look stunning. But little girlfriend, you're so pretty you can get away with any color you choose."

"Uh, thank you," I murmur. I feel weird. She called me *pretty*! I'm trying to pretend I'm chill, but then Anastasia gave me a look that might have said she agreed with her.

I think we're gonna buy this dress.

CHAPTER 60
Dad's Week

DAD HAS SCHEDULED Madame Rubenstein to come three times a week until the recital, to make sure I'm 100 percent ready.

I'm on the bench, fingers arched "just so," as Madame Rubenstein says. I wait for her signal to begin. Usually we start with a repetition of basic scales and chords. But today I can see a hint of a smile on her face. I look at her quizzically.

"I have something to share with you," she says, reaching into her leather bag and pulling out a clunky-looking black machine. I've never seen anything like it. I wait.

"In case you're wondering," she tells me as she fiddles with the buttons on the machine, "this is a cassette player. Not many people use them much anymore. You young people are into downloads and such. *This* is an actual recording of a live performance."

She finds the cord for the cassette player, plugs it in. She then pulls out a small plastic object a little wider than a Post-it note, and she snaps it into the machine. She presses the button marked PLAY and— voilà! (as she would say)—music fills the room. It's my recital piece, Clementi's sonatina, but it's sure not the way it sounds when *I* play! Every note is pure. Every chord is precise. Every passage is perfect.

"Wow! Who is that?" I exclaim. "That's *really* good!"

"His name is Alessandro Deljavan. I met him once in Europe. He is magnificent!"

Then a horrible thought hits me. "Do you expect me to play it like that?" I ask.

"Signor Deljavan pours himself into the music itself. That's all I ask you to do. Feel it. Breathe it."

I think I get what she is trying to tell me. The rest of the lesson goes really well. I'm betting both Mom and Dad will record my performance on their phones.

I wonder what it will sound like when I listen to it.

CHAPTER 61
Mom's Week

OMG! I'M TRYING not to stress out! Pianopalooza is next week! I'll be at Dad's, but I practice madly at Mom's as well—that Casio is sounding really good!

It starts at 5:00 p.m., but all participants have to be there early—by 3:00 at the latest.

It's supposed to last two hours. Ha, ha—all four parents have to stay in the same room for 120 minutes. See one another's faces. Breathe one another's air.

Ha! I love it.

I know that Darren will break his neck to get a seat in the very first row so he can cheer me on. Love that, too! I think I'm gonna like having a big brother!

I keep thinking—an awful lot of really beautiful music will be played at that recital. And I keep hoping that maybe some of that pretty will rub off on my parents—maybe make them continue to be nice to each other for a little while.

Yeah, melodies and harmony. Nice.

CHAPTER 62
Mom's Week

MY CASIO IS doing it's job—take that, Madame Rubenstein!

I discovered a way to listen to the recording of the piece and play at the same time. Measure by measure. Note for note. When I do it right, it's so good it scares me. I'm one with that Clementi dude. I think he'd be proud of me.

Mom just grins as I play. She's happier than I've seen her in a long time. She's no longer working double shifts, and she's getting a lot more rest. At the same time she's, like, supercharged, washing windows and ironing sheets. Who irons sheets? Gee! But I gotta give her credit, she's not letting all her wedding stuff get in the way of my concert. She listens to me practice, reminds me to sit up straight and bend my fingers "just so." I don't tell her, but that really makes me feel good deep inside.

CHAPTER 63
Exchange Day

AT THE MALL today I'm sitting with Mom, waiting for Dad and Anastasia. As I watch for them, who do I see but Clint Hammond and a woman that I guess is his mother, strolling past the Apple Store. He sees me, waves, and walks toward us.

I channel my inner calm.

"Hey," he says, giving me a nod. "What's up?"

"Nothin' much," I say, nodding back.

"Uh, this is my mother," he says.

"Glad to meet you, Mrs. Hammond," I say. I even offer my hand—I know how to be polite to grown-ups!

"And this is *my* mother," I add, tapping my mom's

forearm. Mom's not working today, so she's wearing a pair of black leggings and a white T-shirt decorated with shiny purple hearts. The slogan today says, "Happier than a unicorn eating cake on a rainbow."

The two moms greet each other and—holy moly—they really hit it off. Mom's telling Clint's mother, whose name is Sarah, about some new athletic clothing store opening up next week. And Clint's mom, it seems, is excited about the slime store—something about a birthday present for her niece. They're chatting about T-shirts and slime stuff and legging designers. I had no idea such a job even existed! Mom would be great at that!

While they babble on, I notice Clint's holding a LEGO bag.

"What'd you get?" I ask.

He shrugs. "I picked up a special order from the LEGO store."

"LEGOs? Aren't those for five-year-olds?" I blurt out before I think. Argh!

Clint's eyes flicker as sunlight from the skylight hits his hair just then—it looks almost golden for a second. Shining. I can't believe I just said such a thoughtless thing, and my brain is scrambling to make up for it.

But he tells me, "I go to LEGO competitions

around the country. Around the world, actually." He gets an excited look on his face. "I've been to London and Madrid."

"Competitions? For LEGOs?" I ask, stunned.

"Yeah. We have teams, and we race to see who can assemble the best robotic LEGO creation in the allotted time. It's serious fun."

"Wow! I had no idea. You must have to be a fast thinker, to come up with inventions like that."

"I guess," he says, kinda grinning, but kinda shyly, too.

"I play the piano," I tell him, suddenly feeling kinda shy myself. "I have a competition coming up in a few weeks."

"That's pretty cool," he says. "You any good?"

"Not too shabby," I admit.

Clint looks over at our mothers, who are still going on like they've known each other for years.

"Your mom's really pretty," he says.

"Thanks. It's weird to think of her as pretty—she's just Mom, you know?"

He nods. "You look a lot like her," he adds.

Huh? That's cool—no one ever says I look like my mom.

But then he goes and says, "I had no idea your

mother was white. That's how you get your good looks, I guess."

"Wait." At first I'm not sure what he means. Then it hits me. "What?"

He doesn't stop there. "Mixed kids are always pretty," he adds, pushing his bangs to the side.

My face is going hot. It dawns on me that he hasn't got the foggiest notion of what he just said. So I decide to tell him.

"So . . . you're saying that the pretty part of me came from my mom, and if I weren't pretty, then that would have come from my dad?"

"Uh, that's not what I meant . . . that's not . . . ," he stammers.

His mother is waving bye to Mom and giving Clint the time-to-leave nod. He can't seem to look at me and ends up loping away without even saying good-bye. Then he's gone.

I stare after him, feeling so sad. He didn't have a clue. He had *no* idea how much that hurt. Not a clue.

CHAPTER 64
Dad's Week

PIANOPALOOZA IS TOMORROW! I've been practicing all week, so I'm not going to stress myself about it. What I'm more worried about is the giant zit on my forehead. I've never had a zit before! It's huge, like maybe ten inches across. Well, maybe not that big. Maybe five inches. Maybe one. I stare into the mirror. It's actually just a speck. But it *feels* huge. It *glares* at me.

"What am I gonna do?" I yelp to Anastasia, who comes running into my bathroom. "I might as well have a neon sign on my forehead!"

She does not laugh at me. I give her points for that.

"I know that tiny little bump feels like a mountain to you—" she starts to say.

"I just want the recital to be perfect!" I interrupt. "But now this!" I start to pick at it.

"Don't mess with it," she warns. "You don't want to invite its friends to show up."

"You mean there might be more of them coming?"

"Hmm. I *think* I might have something that can help." She hurries out while the thing continues to grow on my face. It'll be the size of Ohio in a minute. Maybe the whole continent by bedtime!

Anastasia returns with a small brown bottle. "Darren uses this," she explains. "It's called Lucky Tiger— sounds like just what we need, a bit of luck and a dab of cream. Let's just put a little bit of this on." She lets me sniff it when she unscrews the cap. Nice—kinda citrus smelling.

She put a teeny amount on her fingertip, then gently touches it to my face. It feels cool and slightly tingly.

I turn back to the mirror. The red bump is covered with a small dab of white cream. Now, *this* is a look. Not!

"You think this will work?" I ask worriedly.

"It always worked for me," she replies.

"You used to get zits?" I ask her.

"I still do," she tells me. "All faces get irritated from time to time."

"Whoa. That's a bummer!"

"But you teenagers usually get more blemishes because your skin is changing, just like the rest of your body."

Did she just call me a teenager? Well slay me! But I just say, "Thanks for letting me use it."

"Any time," she says.

She opens a compact with a little mirror and pats a bit of her makeup on my face. Yep, not the kid stuff I used to pretend with, but seriously expensive adult woman makeup! Cool!

Then she gives me a hug, a real hug, kinda like a mom-would-give-a-daughter hug. And okay. Fine. It feels pretty good.

CHAPTER 65
Dad's Week

I WAKE UP early—can't even hear the birds yet! And my heart is beating like it did the day I accidentally drank a double-espresso Caramel Frappuccino from Starbucks. I told the lady "heavy on the whipped cream." I think she heard "heavy on the caffeine," and she gave me a double espresso. I didn't figure it out until three in the morning, when I woke Mom to tell her I thought I was having a heart attack.

I gotta wash my hair. And take a shower. Maybe two—just to make sure. Am I out of Whoosh? I hope not. I peer into the mirror. The zit, miraculously, just as Anastasia predicted, seems to be gone.

Just as I'm thinking this is the start of a perfect day, everything goes wacko. I wander into the kitchen for juice and toast.

"I have meetings at the office all day, Isabella," Dad tells me as he grabs a granola bar from the cupboard.

"On a *Saturday*? How come you have to do this *today*?"

"New clients. Big emergency. But don't worry—I'll have them out the door well before the recital."

"Promise?" I stare him down.

"Absolutely promise! Pinkie swear!" He offers me the little finger of his left hand. I lift up mine and our pinkies touch. It's been a long time since we did this. "I will be there by four, when the doors open."

"Okay. You know where to park?"

"I've got you, baby girl." He gives me a quick kiss on my ear. "I will be there—with bells on! Anastasia will get you there by three, okay?"

He's out the door before I can answer.

Like she's the next actor in a scene of a play, Anastasia bustles into the kitchen not a minute after Dad leaves. She's wearing a dark-gray suit and fluffy house slippers. After pouring herself a cup of coffee, she sits down and checks her iPad, then frowns. She looks up at me.

"Excited about the recital today?" she asks.

I take a deep breath. "Yep. Really, really." Am I sensing a "but" coming from her?

"You've been practicing your fingers off—I've been so impressed."

"Thanks." I gulp down the rest of my orange juice.

"Your new shoes fit well?" Anastasia asks. She's quick-slurping her coffee.

"Perfectly!" I tell her. "Boy, they really have that shine working! Almost as shiny as the bangle Madame Rubenstein gave me. I'm going to wear that, too. Maybe it will bring me good luck."

"You don't need luck, honey. You are prepared and perfect!"

Darren slides into the room next, still damp from the shower. He's wearing way too much musk cologne. So Darren.

"You trying to fumigate the place?" I fake choke and wave my hands to clear the air.

"Just wanna be fresh for the ladies!" he says, grabbing the last doughnut.

"Darren, would you be able to drive Isabella to the recital?" Anastasia asks then. "I just found out that I have an early showing of one of the houses I designed this afternoon, for one of my biggest clients.

I'll meet you at the university by four."

"Sure, Mom," he says. "Not a problem. I like hanging out with our very own piano prodigy."

I give him a poke on the shoulder.

"Love you, Isabella!" Anastasia calls as she slides off her slippers and slips on her heels. She tucks her iPad in her briefcase and hurries out the door. "See you at four o'clock," she calls out. "Promise."

"Love you, too," I respond automatically. Then it strikes me that I've actually never said that to her. I think about it. I guess I really have come to love her. I see Anastasia bite down on a huge smile as she closes the front door. Ha—playing it cool!

I gather the kitchen dishes, put them in the sink, and wipe the table and countertops with some lemon-smelling spray stuff. As I wash and rinse, Darren dries.

"So, you gonna practice all day?" he asks as he puts the dishes in the cupboard.

"No, I don't think so. It's in my head. It's in my heart. When I sit down to play, it will pour out of me. That's the plan, at any rate."

"That's kinda how I feel before a basketball game. I feel it, you know? It's in me, waiting to burst out."

Fifi wanders into the kitchen, her polished nails—silver today—clicking against the tiled floor. She stops by my chair, then scooches back on her hind legs and reaches out to me. She never comes to me! I touch her head tentatively. Her fur is so silky. Then she click-click-clicks away.

"Even the psycho dog is on your side today," Darren observes.

I shrug, but yeah, it is kinda amazing.

"So when are your mother and John Mark getting to the recital hall?" Darren asks.

"Oh, they'll be the first ones there, for sure. They both took the day off, just so they can be super early. Mom wants to grab a front-row seat. She's so excited! She told me she's been charging her phone all night so she has enough juice to record me while I'm playing."

"That's what mamas do!" Darren says.

"I gotta go take a shower," I tell him, touching my hair.

"I thought you just got out of the shower!" he says.

"I did. But it's the only thing that calms me down. I may be half tuna fish before it's time to leave!"

CHAPTER 66
Dad's Week

IT'S A LITTLE after 2:00 p.m. Even though I told Darren I wasn't going to practice, I played my recital piece, like, seventeen times. Then maybe seventeen more. The notes on the page are practically etched inside my head. I bet even when I'm an old-lady grandma, I will be able to play this piece of music perfectly.

I have taken four showers in total. And my hair's not gonna move till next week! I've slicked it with super-hold gel and dared even one strand to jump out of place. After I get dressed, I slide Madame Rubenstein's bangle on my arm and gaze in the mirror. I look like a . . . a pianist. Not a kid, not a student, but a professional piano player, ready for a concert performance. And I feel like a contender.

I run my hands over the soft velvet of my dress, smoothing any unseen wrinkles, and I happily discover it has hidden pockets! Perfect. I slip my phone into the right-hand one. I spin around. Not bad. Not bad at all! I'm ready.

Darren's in the living room playing a game on his phone when I come downstairs. He looks up and whistles. "Man, you look real pretty, little-sister-to-be," he says. "You'll be the best-looking, most talented, and cleanest kid in the whole recital!"

I give him a formal curtsy. "Thank you, monsieur," I say, using my best fake French accent. I'm actually blushing. Nobody's ever really complimented me like *that* before. I feel like giving the whole world a big hug. I am so ready for this.

"Well, it's true. Given the amount of time I've heard you practicing, I'm a pretty good judge." He turns on his phone and snaps a few photos. I can't help but cheese.

I grab my black music portfolio even though I won't need it. Everything at a recital is performed from memory. I got this!

"You think we can leave a little early?" I ask.

"Maybe we can grab a smoothie or something."

"You hungry?"

"Not really. Just hyped." I'm spinning around in the living room.

"Chill, kid. You're gonna be amazing!"

I give him a fist bump. I'm just so psyched. "Can we leave a little early anyway? I just can't wait one more second!" So much for chill! Ha!

"Probably a good idea," he says, laughing. "I don't want to watch you implode right here in the living room. Besides, traffic by the university is always crazy. Give me a few secs to get out of these sweats, and we're on the road."

When he comes back, it's my turn to whistle. In a burgundy suede blazer, a crisp white shirt, and slim-fitting beige pants, Darren's definitely got his mama's fashion flair.

"You don't look so bad yourself!" I tell him. "You clean up pretty good!"

He checks himself out in the hallway mirror.

"I can't help it if I'm fine," he replies, his turn to cheese. "Let's split."

"Banana split?" I joke. We both laugh. Then I'm thinking, *Mmmm, ice cream.*

So I put on my brightest smile, the one I hope says,

You can't resist, and I ask, "Hmm, I don't suppose we can stop and get ice cream on the way, can we?"

"You're a mess, girl," Darren says as he grabs his phone. "What if you get it on your new dress?"

"Uh, I didn't think about that."

Darren runs to the kitchen and is back a second later with a folded linen towel.

"You're the best," I tell him, taking it.

"Ready?" he asks.

I nod. "Let's do this thing."

I am so relieved. It is time.

We hurry out the front door, and I slide into the backseat of his car. Two more years, Mom told me, and I can ride in the front.

As I strap on my seat belt, I ask hopefully, "Can we go to Graeter's? This is an important day. It deserves the best ice cream!"

"As you wish, m'lady," he says as he backs out of the driveway.

I rub the leather music portfolio on my lap and take a deep breath.

The sky is blue.

I know my piece.

I'm ready.

CHAPTER 67
Dad's Week

PARKING IS ALWAYS tricky in front of Graeter's, especially on a sunny Saturday afternoon. The area is called Hyde Park Square, but it's really more like an oval, with cool stores nestled together. Darren and I luck out—he eases into a spot across from the Key Bank, just a couple of doors away.

As we are getting out of the car, I get a text from Dad.

You okay? Almost there? Got your music? I'm leaving now. See you soon. Love you!

I text him back that all is well, skip the fact that we're stopping for ice cream—he'll worry about ice cream on my dress! As I'm slipping the phone back into my pocket, I get a text from Mom, all hyped up.

I can't wait to hear you play, sweetie! John Mark is gonna record it all so I can take pix! So proud of you, Izzy.

Then Darren's phone buzzes—a text from Anastasia. We smirk.

He reads it out loud. "'Leaving now. Is Isabella calm and prepared? Drive safely. See you soon. Love you.'"

He texts her back, and we hurry into the magic that is Graeter's Ice Cream. Graeter's has been around for, like, a million years, and the ice cream is not just fantastic, but famous—even been mentioned on TV shows and stuff. Apparently, people from as far away as New York order it!

The choices are incredible, and new ones are created every month. Blueberry Delight. Vienna Coffee. Bourbon Pecan Chocolate Chip. Boysenberry. Peppermint Stick. All made here in town. Every time I walk in here, I shiver from the anticipation of the deliciousness to come. I can almost inhale the feeling of the place. It's got atmosphere. There's that word again. I swear that man lives inside my head!

I check out the other customers. Nobody seems to notice how dressed up we are today. But that's cool—Mom and I once actually came here in our pj's late one night! Nobody said anything then, either.

I look over the new listings. Instead of my usual Oregon Strawberry, I switch for two dips of Madagascar Vanilla Bean on a waffle cone. It sounds fancy and exotic. Darren orders Double Chocolate Chip. The teenager behind the counter stuffs the cones extra full. "Enjoy!" she says with a smile as she hands them to us.

Darren steers me by the elbow toward the door. "Let's eat these in the car—Mom'll kill me if I get you there late, so . . ."

"And then *my* mom'll kill you a second time," I say with a laugh as I hold the door open for him.

"Thank you, Your Piano-ness!" he says with a bow, cracking me up.

As we head to the car, I take a giant bite of my ice cream—I love the fire-hot/cold on my teeth. Then I lick around the edges so it doesn't drip. Darren double-clicks his key fob to unlock the car doors.

Then, from out of nowhere, a man with stringy reddish-blond hair, in a dark brown T-shirt, sprints toward us from the other side of the street. His face looks fierce. He bumps directly into Darren, who yells, "Hey! Watch where you're going, dude!" as his chocolate cone falls to the ground. *Oh no! His ice cream!* I know he wants to curse, but he doesn't. Because of me.

The man ignores him, dashes past us, and disappears behind a building.

"What the heck?" Darren asks, rubbing his shoulder.

"That guy was so rude!" I cry out. "You okay? You want some of my vanilla bean?"

"Forget about it—I'm cool," Darren says, getting into the car. He gives his head a quick shake as if to clear it. "Let's just get you to Pianopalooza. Who invented that crazy name, anyway?" He's trying to get back to our happy place, I can tell. He checks his rearview mirror as I buckle in, then carefully backs out of the parking spot. As he drives slowly down the crowded street, he turns on his latest playlist—he likes jazz. I check the clock on the dashboard—it's only two fifteen. We've got plenty of time. I pull the kitchen towel in different directions so it covers my entire dress, and slowly lick that Madagascar Vanilla Bean yumminess. We'll be there in fifteen minutes.

"Sure you don't want a bite?" I ask, holding out my cone.

"Naw, I'm good. It's chocolate or die, for me!"

Come to think of it, he *does* always order chocolate when we go places. Good to know.

We aren't halfway down the block when I'm vaguely aware of the multicolored flashing lights behind us.

Darren notices too, because he says, "Something bad must have happened. Look at all these cop cars!"

Then I hear the sirens. "A fire, maybe?" I say.

I stretch around to look out the back window. I see a sea of red and blue. There have to be a dozen police cars behind us. People are stopping on the sidewalk to stare.

Darren slows down and looks for a place to pull over so they can go by, but there are no parking places. Then I hear something that sounds like the megaphone that the coach uses when we're in gym class. "Pull over! Pull over now!"

"Who's he talking to?" I ask Darren. I'm looking around, trying to figure out what the problem is.

"I have no idea," Darren tells me. But he stops anyway, right in the middle of the street. There is no place else to go.

A black-gloved fist suddenly pounds on Darren's window. Darren jumps in his seat. I scream. "Get out of the car!" an angry voice demands.

"Are they talking to *me*?" Darren asks, his voice quavering.

"I said, get out of the car. Now!" The angry voice is even angrier. He gives the window another wallop. *Is car glass breakable?* I think crazily.

Then another fist pounds on *my* window in the back. "Open this door and get out! Hands in the air!" I hear.

Me? My hands are shaking so hard I can hardly press the unlock button. I look wildly at Darren to see if he thinks I should get out, but as he opens his own door, he's yanked right off his seat. He nearly falls, but a cop grabs his arm. Darren thrusts his other arm up in the air.

What is happening? I don't know what to do. My decision is made for me. The back door is flung open and someone grabs me, roughly, and pulls me out— literally pulls me out of the car. *What's going on? Hey! My ice cream!* The towel falls to the ground, and the ice-cream cone slides down my dress, my black velvet dress.

CHAPTER 68
Dad's Week

NOW I AM being pushed toward the front of the car. "Don't move! Don't even breathe," I am told. *Don't breathe? How do you* not *breathe? Will the police shoot me because I don't know how to stop breathing?* I don't even know why I'm thinking this. But then I'm thinking about Darren. *Where is Darren?*

I look around for him and see instead a female officer approaching me with her gun out. It is aimed at me. A gun is aimed at my head! And now I *can't* breathe!

And there's Darren. He's on the ground. *On the sidewalk!* At least three policemen are on top of him, his burgundy blazer barely visible. The policemen who are not holding him down have their guns drawn. Aimed at Darren.

They are all bellowing different things. "Stop resisting! Don't move!"

Darren couldn't possibly move even one finger. They have him pinned down. I think he's handcuffed! *Handcuffed?*

He's answering; his voice is muffled. "I did not do anything, sir."

"Where were you ten minutes ago?"

"At Graeter's. Buying ice cream," comes his muffled reply.

"When did you go into the bank?"

"Bank? What bank?"

"You were seen running from the Key Bank!"

"And leaving in a red car!"

"Please let me stand up," Darren says. I can hear tears in his voice. "Please. Sir."

"Where is the money?"

"What?"

I feel like my ears are hearing another language or something. And some lady is still pointing her gun at me! I want to say he just bought me an ice cream—but they told me not to breathe and that means no talking and why is she pointing that gun and I want her to put it down and Darren is standing again and he's bleeding . . . Darren is bleeding, and his arms are pulled behind his back because he actually *is* in handcuffs. He is crying.

I finally hear something I understand.

"I have a receipt for the ice cream," Darren says slowly. "Look in my jacket pocket." *If Darren is allowed to talk, then maybe I can breathe.* So I do.

An officer approaches him like he's a serial killer or something and slowly reaches into the pocket of Darren's sport coat, which is now ripped at one shoulder.

Burgundy is the color of blood pops into my head.

The policeman pulls out a wrinkled slip of paper. He shakes it in Darren's face.

"This doesn't prove you didn't rob that bank!" the officer yells.

"Rob a bank?" Darren says, gaping. "I never even went into the bank!"

"Your car was seen leaving the scene!"

"It . . . it was the only parking space available near the ice-cream store!" Darren replies. He's suddenly starting to sound angry, even though I know he's trying to stay calm.

The woman with the gun still has it aimed at me. Darren notices. "That's my little sister. I was taking her to a piano recital! She's eleven! Are you nuts?"

No one answers, but the officer lowers her gun. She does not, however, put it in her holster.

"We saw a man running," I whisper, my voice so shaky I don't recognize it as my own.

"What man?" the lady officer demands. She raises her gun a little tick.

"He had on a dark-colored shirt. He ran behind that restaurant," I tell them. I can only move my head. I'm too scared to lift my arm to point.

"I saw him too!" Darren exclaims. "He bumped into me, made me drop my ice cream."

"What did he look like?" another officer asks.

"Reddish-blond hair. Skinny. Pimply face. Brown T-shirt."

The policemen take notes. They talk to one another. They talk into their shoulders, where their walkie-talkies are located. One of them jogs back to the bank.

Time has stopped.

I stand there, needing to scratch my nose. I am afraid to move. The itch intensifies.

They let us stand there. Darren, surrounded by men in blue who speak around him but not to him.

No one says a word to me. We wait. And wait. *I want my mom. I want my dad.*

The guns are still in the policemen's hands. Real guns. Black and shiny and terrifyingly close.

The officer who headed to the bank now jogs back. "The bank employees say the robber was a thin white man. Another witness said he thought the man got into a red car."

"Well, I'm not a skinny white man," Darren says slowly, reasonably. "I'm as brown as that ice cream he made me drop. You can see it, on the ground, over there." He nods in the direction we came from. "And we simply parked in front of the bank because there were no other spaces," he explains again. "My license and registration are in the glove compartment."

Another officer saunters over. "The bank confirms the robber did not look like this suspect," he says.

So why did they do this to us? Why? I'm screaming in my head.

And finally, after what seems like fifty hours, they remove Darren's handcuffs. He rubs his wrists. They must really hurt. Then they tell him not to move. He stops rubbing.

At least the situation seems to be calming down. People in the crowd are losing interest and walking away. Will they let us go now? Then a thought flashes through my brain. *The concert! Oh no! The concert! I'm going to be late! Mom and Dad are gonna be so worried that I'm not there yet! I've got to call them!* So I reach into my pocket for my phone.

The lady officer yells, "Gun! Gun!"

Every point of light I've ever known explodes at that moment.

Honey-gold sun.

Turquoise sky.

Flaming-red pain.

I collapse to the ground. The last things I remember hearing are Darren's hoarse scream and a male voice shouting, "Shots fired! Shots fired! Send emergency medical crews ASAP."

CHAPTER 69
Dad's Week

I HIT THE ground with a thud and a throb. *Owww!*
I think my head bounces. The back of it hurts *so* bad.
Cement is *hard*! I hear lots of shouting and screaming—
seems like it's coming from a tunnel. Are those wails
coming from Darren? Why is the sky slanted?

Confusing voices surround me.

"Dispatch, this is car seven-two-four. We have a
ten-forty-three-A. Shots fired. We need a medical
team. I repeat. Shots fired. Victim is a child—a girl
aged ten or eleven."

I want to tell that voice I'm almost twelve. But I
can't get the words in my head out of my mouth. Why

is my arm on fire? And my head! *Oh, my head! It hurts so bad!*

Someone dressed in blue hovers over me. *He needs to brush his teeth! Man, his breath reeks!* He touches my arm. I scream. He leans closer and touches my chest with something my doctor uses—a stethoscope? *Why? What's going on?* All I can think is that my head *hurts!*

"We've got a lot of blood here."

Blood? My blood? From what?

"Where's the gun?"

Are they talking about me? *What gun?*

"She had no gun. The only thing in her pocket is a cell phone."

My phone. I need to call my mom. She's gonna be mad if I miss the recital.

"Are you sure?"

"Yes, sir. Just a phone."

I'm so confused. I want Mom. Why is my arm burning so bad?

My arm. My head. I open my eyes and look up. I think I'm lying on the ground. Someone lifts my arm and wraps something around it. A howl sound. Is that me? *Leave my arm alone. You're hurting me.*

I am lifted.

I'm so dizzy.

Colors swirl.

I'm placed on a flat, bedlike thing. I'm outside. Why am I on a bed outside? I feel movement, like I'm being rolled. I am lifted again. Pushed.

I can see a ceiling. Where am I? A lady in a white uniform smiles at me. I throw up all over her.

Everything fades to dark.

CHAPTER 70
Dad's Week

I AM AWAKE inside my head before I open my eyes. It is safe here in the dark with my eyes closed. I can hear a faint beeping not far from me. And a soft whoosh.

I am lying flat. I'm on a bed, but it's not my bed at either house. I touch the sheets. Rough. Not from Anastasia's house. Not Mom's, either.

I sniff. The air smells too clean, too perfect. I do not know this place. I wiggle my toes. They seem to work.

I try to lift my arms, but only the left one moves. My entire right arm seems to be attached to the bed. I feel pinned down like a bug. I start to panic.

A soft voice filters through my fear. "Hi, honey. You

awake?" I do not know this voice. Now I'm scared.

"Open your eyes, sweetie. Relax. It's okay. You're fine."

I blink. I hear the same noises—the beeping, the whooshing. But it's dark, shadowy. I can't make out anything clearly.

"My name is Naomi, and I'm a nurse," the soft voice says. "I've been waiting for you to wake up."

I can't form a full sentence. My head feels like it's full of sand. And rocks. And the back of it is throbbing, throbbing. I want to lie down, but I'm already lying down.

"Where . . . ?" I try to say. I'm gulping on nothing. "What . . . ?"

"Sh-sh-sh," she says. "Relax. You're at Good Samaritan Hospital. And you're gonna be just fine."

I try to sit up, but oh boy, my head feels like it's going to burst wide open. The woman gently places her hand on my chest. "Let's not try to move too much just yet, okay?"

I ease back down, and it's like the rocks in my brain shift around and let pieces of thoughts trickle out. Ice cream. Police cars. Sunlight. Handcuffs. A gun? Darren . . . did he fall? Where was Darren? *Where was Darren?*

"Where's Darren?" I ask, fear in my throat.

"He's here. Along with a whole bunch of moms and dads who have been itching to get in here and see you. I kept them out so you could get yourself together first."

"Thank you," I say.

Weird. If I keep my eyes closed, it hurts less to talk.

I open one eye slowly. "Darren's not hurt?"

"He's got a few scrapes and bruises, but he's perfectly fine."

"You sure?"

"I checked him myself. He's fine. Trust me."

I am suddenly ridiculously thirsty. "Can I have some water?" I ask.

"Shall we try to sit up, just a little?" she asks.

No, but I'm so thirsty. So I nod and open my eyes just a teeny bit. She pushes a button that eases the bed up so I'm in an almost-sitting position and I don't have to do a thing. But no joke—for sure, any minute now, my head will truly explode.

The room starts spinning—worse than the time I rode the Tilt-A-Whirl twice. My head throbs and pulses. *Ohhh. That hurts!* Is it possible for a human head to detonate?

I want to lie back flat. But I want water more. So I don't complain about my head.

The nurse takes a Styrofoam cup with a bendy straw from a little table I did not notice. She holds it to my lips. I suck it greedily.

My right arm throbs from the movement. I wince and gaze at it in confusion. White, gauzy-looking stuff covers my upper arm. It hurts like crazy.

And my head is pounding. Everything is distorted. Wobbly. Not really real. *Oh man, this hurts!*

But I take a deep breath. "Am I okay?"

"Absolutely," the nurse assures me. And suddenly a whole rush of questions crowd my mind. Like, how did I end up in the hospital? And why did this happen? And am I in trouble?

I touch my head and wince.

"That's going to be tender for a couple of days. But you'll be fine. I promise," the nurse says gently as she pushes a button to make the bed go flat again.

I try to breathe slowly. Maybe that'll help. Memories streak into my head. "There was a gun," I say with confusion. "A real gun! And noise. And fire on my arm. And then my head . . ."

I give up. Thinking is too hard. Pain echoes through my skull like drum beats.

"Shhhh. You've had a rough afternoon. But you're just fine."

"Can you . . . can you tell me what happened?" I can't get my thoughts to stay still.

Naomi pauses. "You ready for all this?"

I close my eyes again—better. "Yeah, I think so."

"I don't know all the details about what happened with your brother and the police, but you came in with a gunshot wound to the arm."

"I got shot?!" I got *shot*? By a *gun*? I blink my eyes open to see if she is for real.

"I'm afraid so, honey. It seems you reached for a cell phone, and a police officer, well, she thought you were reaching for a gun."

"I'm eleven! Where would I get a gun?" I demand, wincing. *Argh, my head!*

"Crazy, I know. I don't ask those kinds of questions. I'm only here to patch up the wounds," she tells me. "Anyway, the officer's gun went off—she says it was an accident—and your arm was hit."

I ponder this information. "I have a bullet in my arm?" I ask finally. And then, because I've seen way too many murder mysteries on TV with my mom, I whisper, "Am I going to die?"

"No, sweetie. You're good. Honest. Fortunately, the officer was a lousy shot. Or maybe you moved at just the right moment. The bullet tore through your skin, and a couple of layers beneath that, but luckily didn't hit bone. You got what we'd call a bad graze. Your body jumped into save-Isabella mode, and you'll be fine."

"Do I have stitches?"

"No. Not a one! But you'll have quite a scar to show your friends when you go back to school."

"So why am I in the hospital?"

"According to the ambulance report, you fell and hit your head pretty hard when you were shot. You were knocked out. Not from the bullet, but from the sidewalk. You have a pretty bad concussion."

I touch the back of my head with my left hand—the arm that's not bandaged. I can feel that my hair is a big tangle. "Ow!" I cry out. I don't care what my hair's doing—I'm not touching my head again. Not for a couple of years at least!

"What's your pain level, one to ten?" Nurse Naomi asks.

"I guess an eight," I tell her. "It's pretty bad."

"Okay, I'll see if I can get you some ibuprofen."

"What's that?"

"Basically, it's fancy aspirin," she tells me with a pleasant laugh. "It will help ease the pain."

I nod, but I stop real quick—yeouch!

"What's all this stuff on my arm?" I ask her next.

"We put in an IV—stands for 'intravenous'—it's pretty standard procedure, to make sure you're getting enough fluids."

"You're putting water into my arm?"

"Nope. It's a saline and dextrose solution."

"What's that?"

"Basically, salt and sugar!" she says, chuckling as she types notes into a laptop on the side table.

But then I gasp and sit straight up. *Oww!* "Oh no! What time is it?"

"Nine p.m. You got somewhere to be, sweetie?"

I slump back on the pillow. "Not anymore."

Nine at night? How can it be? Then I'm wondering what happened to that pretty black dress.

Nurse Naomi fluffs my pillow. "Are you ready to let me bring in all those folks in the waiting room?" she asks.

"Are they fighting and yelling at each other?"

She tilts her head. "No. . . . I actually saw them holding hands. And praying at one point."

"Praying? You gotta be kidding me."

"Heads bowed. Hands locked. I kid you not."

I'm having trouble believing this is even possible. "Seriously? All four of them?"

"Five, including your brother. Looks like you have a nice blended family."

"You have no idea," I tell her with a half smile.

She places a warmed blanket on my bed—wow, that feels good—and pulls it close around my neck.

"Tragedy often brings togetherness," she says. "I've seen it happen here a million times."

I nod again—ooh, gotta stop doing that—and reach for more water.

"Can I have a little more time alone before you let them in?" I ask her, then take a sip. "And maybe a cookie or something, please? I'm starving!"

"You got it, kid!" Naomi taps my unbandaged arm gently, then strides out of the room.

I lie there in the whiteness of that room and let my thoughts do the walking.

Snippets of unplayed piano music.

Ropes and nooses.

Random vocabulary words.

The color green.

Anastasia—who names their kid Anastasia, anyway?

Her stupid little dog.

John Mark. Big trucks.

Darren.

Cinnamon rolls.

Police cars.
Weddings.
Guns.
Sunlight.
Shadows.
Too much to figure out. My head hurts. My arm—
oh, my arm. I just want to sleep a little more. So I do.

CHAPTER 71
Dad's Week

THERE'S A SOFT knock on the door. Then a head peeps through the narrow opening. It's Darren. "Want a visitor?" he asks, his voice low and soothing.

I try to nod, but my head still does not seem to like movement. "Just you right now, okay?"

He steps back out. I can hear more whispers.

Then Darren comes in and closes the door behind him. He has a two-inch bandage taped to the side of his forehead. He's still wearing that awesome burgundy blazer, but it's ripped on one side, splattered with . . . blood.

As he gets closer, I can see scrapes and welts on his face.

I burst into tears.

He runs to me and grabs my free hand. "Hey, hey, Izzy, Izzy," he murmurs, "it's okay. It's *okay*."

I reach for his face. "They hurt you!"

"Nah. They tried to, but I'm pretty tough."

"Why aren't you in a hospital room like me?"

"I just have a couple of scrapes and bruises," he explains. "Nothing earth shattering. Remember that song called 'Dirt off Your Shoulder'?"

I nod, then stifle a giggle. "It's got cusswords in it!"

"Yeah, it's clearly not in your lane, but the whole thing is about not letting bad stuff eat you up." But his jaw clenches; he turns and crosses the room to the one window. The streetlights are on.

"What can you see?" I ask him after a bit.

"Cars. Trees. Streets. People doing whatever."

"I bet lots of them have had terrible stuff happen to them."

"You're pretty smart for an eleven-year-old." He pivots and comes back to sit on the side of my bed.

"Almost twelve," I remind him, cheesing. Then I squeeze my eyes shut. Memories of today snarl my thoughts. My smile dissolves.

"We're gonna get through this," he says. "You and me. Together."

"So you say," I mutter. "Hard to do." I stare at the far wall—it's painted a dull blue. Now, if they'd had *me* as a room designer, I would have made it lots more cheerful. Yellow, maybe. With spots of orange.

But we have blue, so we gaze at that dull wall. A monitor behind me makes regular beeping noises.

"Are you . . . were you . . . no, are you scared? Or angry?" I ask him, my voice low and serious.

His eyes crinkle at the corners, but his voice is hard. "I gotta admit—I'm still pretty freaked out." He pauses, looks quickly at the door, then back to me. "I feel like there's somebody behind me. Kinda . . . jumpy, ya know."

"I feel ya."

He pulls a hunk of tissues out of the box beside my bed, squeezes them into a tight ball. He tosses the Kleenex ball into the trash, then yanks out another stack, wads those up, and slam-dunks those into the basket with the others.

"You're killin' my Kleenex, ya know," I tell him as he grabs for more. "I might need to sneeze or something."

Darren's belly laugh is better than medicine. "You're the best, Izzy/Isabella!" Then he fist-bumps my right hand gently—the one at the end of my gauze-wrapped arm. "You and me, kid. We're one. You know that, don't you?"

"For sure!"

"I know the adults in your life have not made it easy."

"Preach," I agree.

"But you're the toughest kid I know," he tells me. "You've handled their mess like a champ. And you'll handle this the same way. You're so much stronger than you think."

"Maybe," I concede. "What about *you*, Darren?"

He starts on another tissue ball—squeezing and squeezing. "It's gonna take some time," he says thoughtfully.

"I . . . Darren—I thought we were gonna die." And now I'm crying again.

"I gotta tell ya, the thought did cross my mind as I was lying there on the ground," he admits. He stands up and stretches. "But we didn't, Izzy. We didn't die. We're good." He turns his head to gaze back at the window.

"Are the cops here? Did they . . . like, apologize?" I ask.

He laughs, harsh. "No. Not to me. They asked me a bunch of stupid questions like I was a criminal or something. They even asked about you—like maybe you always kept guns hidden in the pockets of your recital dresses!" I can see his hands tightening into fists. He blinks real hard.

"Hey, you okay?" I ask.

"No, not really."

"They were so wrong." I bite at my lip. "So, so, so wrong."

"Yep." He pauses. "But I did see that they put the lady cop who shot you in the back of a police car. She was crying."

"Good."

"After the ambulance took you away, some of the cops tried to make like they were still looking for somebody, but it was just an act. About ten minutes later one of them told me that I was free to go. But I didn't know what to do. So I called Dad and Anastasia, then I called your mom and John Mark. Talk about a mess! All four of them were freakin' out!"

"I missed the recital." I'm scared I'm about to ugly-cry. Nope. I sniff hard. Not gonna do that.

"The folks there missed a treat."

"Am I in trouble?"

"For what?" he asks, sounding surprised.

"If I hadn't wanted that stupid ice cream . . . if I hadn't . . ."

And the floodgates open! I cry and cry.

And of course that's when the door opens with a whoosh of light and sound.

Mom's arms are both sweaty and cold. She's shaking so hard she can barely grab me. I reach up with my good arm and pull her to me. She smells like . . . like Mom. We're both sobbing. I'm getting snot on her dress.

Dad runs to the other side of the bed and bends over so close. He needs a shave. This is the first time in my entire life I've ever seen him cry.

The three of us, for just a few moments, are one.

CHAPTER 72
Dad's Week

THE REST OF the evening is filled with too many questions, not so many answers, and . . . ice cream!

All of my families—oh man, I guess I've got multiples (ha, ha)—have crowded into the tiny room. They all want to keep petting me. I feel like a kitten.

My head is still pulsing with pain.

And they all talk at the same time, all babbling mostly the same thing.

"Izzy!" (Mom and John Mark)

"Isabella!" (Dad and Anastasia)

"Are you sure you're okay?" (Mom and Dad)

"Does it hurt?" (John Mark)

"What do you need?" (Anastasia)

"How do you feel?" (Mom)

"Are you in pain?" (Mom and Anastasia)

"How could this happen?" (Dad and John Mark)

"I've already called a lawyer!" (Dad)

"I'm going down to that police station!" (John Mark)

"How dare they?" (Anastasia)

"Oh, my sweet girl!" (Dad)

"My precious, precious darling baby girl." (Mom, of course!)

"Are you in pain?" (Mom and Anastasia, *again*)

Finally Darren hollers out over the din, "Hey! Give her a break!" This shushes them all.

But Mom continues to stroke my face. Dad, too.

Darren places something cold in my good hand. I lift it up and grin. "An ice-cream sandwich!" *Yes!* "Where the heck did you find this?"

"From the vending machine downstairs. It's a little melty, and not Madagascar Vanilla Bean, but it's the best I could do in a hurry."

"Can you open it for me?"

Swiftly he rips open the red-white-and-blue paper wrapping and hands it back. I lick the edges of the fake-tasting vanilla first, then bite into the coolness that's surrounded by that yummy chocolate wafer. *Ahhhhhh.*

Everybody kinda stops talking, and they all smile goofily as they watch me devour the ice-cream sandwich. Is this what two-year-olds feel like when parents watch every little thing they do like it's the best thing since fried rice? Jeesh.

Mom helps me wipe my fingers when I finish, and I lean back on the pillow with satisfaction.

"Do I have to stay here tonight?" I ask.

"Yes, sweetie," Mom tells me. "The doctors just want to keep an eye on you because of the concussion."

"Good," I reply, "'cause I'm sleepy."

I'm glad they figure out I've had enough and need some peace and quiet. Dad and Anastasia come to the bed, and each one kisses me on the cheek—Dad on the left, Anastasia on the right. They hug me once more and promise to be back first thing in the morning.

John Mark and Darren are right behind them. John Mark puts his arm around Darren and hugs him tightly as they walk out the door. Unbelievable!

Mom's staying. I'm so glad. She's going to sleep on a sofa bed I didn't even notice against the back wall of the room. Nurse Naomi brings in a blanket for her.

Before I fall asleep, I ask Mom, "Will I still be able to play the piano?"

"Absolutely," she tells me, squeezing my good hand.

"You sure? My brain's still gonna remember all my songs, all my music, all my melodies?" My voice cracks with worry. I don't want to cry. Again.

"Yes, sweetie. Your head is pretty tough. It will keep all your memories safe. I promise."

She scoots next to me on the bed and holds me close.

I don't tell her about the memories I want to erase.

CHAPTER 73
Exchange Day

WHEN I WAKE up this morning, I find the coolest thing on my bed! A brand-new case to hold my sheet music! Wow—it's the softest leather! It even *smells* good!

Inside is a book of piano music called *Boogies, Ballads, and Beats*. A note from Darren is tucked inside. He wrote, "You rock, Izzy. Hope this music rocks you, too! Love, Darren."

He's the best brother.

Well, the Apple Store will miss me today. Nurse Naomi tells me I'll be here for at least another day—my head still hurts too much when I sit up. When they let me out, it will be Mom's week, so I guess she will take me home. I know she's pleased about that.

CHAPTER 74
Exchange Day

A NEW NURSE strolls in. It's hard to keep up. He writes his name on the whiteboard on the wall: Ian Addington.

"I've never had a man nurse before," I tell him, keeping my voice low as Mom is still asleep.

"You need me to put on lipstick?" he asks, full of fake attitude.

"Might look ridiculous with your beard," I reply, laughing.

"I'm willing to try!" He gives me "meds," as he calls the pills, in a little white paper cup and takes my "vitals" and records it all in a laptop.

"How'm I doing?" I ask.

He answers my question with a question. "How do you feel?"

"Better," I say honestly. "My head doesn't hurt quite as much."

"Good!" he says. He types way more words than I just said, but I guess that's his job. "The doctor will be in to see you shortly. But first I'm removing those bandages!"

"Really?"

"Yep. You're doing just fine. How about a couple of Band-Aids instead of all that gauze? And you don't need this IV anymore either."

"That would be amazing," I tell him with a sigh of relief.

I shut my eyes, but it doesn't hurt when the needle for the IV is removed.

"Can I look at it?" I ask Ian when he lifts off the bandages from my arm.

"Well, sure!"

The wound is reddish, about two inches long, a little swollen, with what's going to be a scab starting to cover it. I've probably had uglier wounds from falling off my bike. Still, *I've got a bullet wound!* It's a little scary. I can't even think what "it" is—and I'm not sure I want to. I'm surprised all I need is a small bandage to cover the spot. I look at my arm for a long time. Man, I got shot! *Shot!* That's really kinda hard to make my brain understand.

"Can I take a shower?" I finally ask.

"You bet," he replies. "But let your mom keep an eye on you to make sure you're steady and balanced, okay?"

"Okay, I will."

He brings me a stack of towels. "Push that red button if you need me, okay?" He hurries out the door.

I look to my left at Mom, curled up tight on the sofa, covered by a thin blanket. She's still wearing the fancy dress she bought for Pianopalooza. I bet she stayed awake most of the night, watching me.

She wakes when she hears the nurse leaving, and bounds barefoot over to my bed. "How you doin', Izzy baby?" she coos as she feels my forehead. What is it with moms and feeling foreheads? Her face is flushed, and her hair is a hot mess.

"I'm okay. Feeling better. Honest," I tell her. "The nurse said I can have a shower. I feel like it's been a million years since my last one."

"Let's do that, then! Your dad and Anastasia and John Mark and Darren will be here soon, I imagine." She fluffs her own hair. "They're probably already pounding at the front door of this place!"

I nod. My head still throbs when I move it, but not as bad as before. "Mom?" I ask as I raise my bed up to a sitting position.

"Yes, sweetie?"

"When we finish the shower, can you run home and bring me some real clothes, please? This hospital stuff is just plain nasty!"

She laughs and laughs. "You *are* feeling better!"

CHAPTER 75
Exchange Day

I FINALLY GET to check my phone. Heather. Imani. Kids I barely even know have sent me messages. How do they even have my number?

Stuff like "Hang in there!" and "We've got your back!" It's a little mind-boggling how nice people are, folks I don't even know.

Jontay sent me a message with a meme of one of the African princesses from the Black Panther movie. It says, "Your power is within you." I like that.

Surprisingly, there's even one from Clint Hammond: Hope ur not mad at me. sorry. really. I prayed for you and your fam. feel better.

Well, now.

Messages from my friends are pretty normal, but I even get a text from Mr. Kazilly! Wow. It was so *very* Kazilly-like! His note said, May your convalescence be brief and your rejuvenation be powerful! Of *course* he used big words! But it was awfully nice of him to send it.

And all those news apps that Mr. K. taught us to use are blowing up with what happened to Darren and me. USA Today. NYTimes.

Me and Darren. We're a trending story on Twitter—probably Facebook, too. We're the headline article of the Sunday newspaper, which is still dropped off at thousands of homes in Cincinnati. And online for those who don't get the paper.

Activists are screaming. Police brutality. Child endangerment. And apparently, Black Lives Matter has put me at the top of its list! I think about that one for a minute.

Plus, NBC News has left a message on my phone? No way. I can't believe this. I scroll down. There's also a message from Black Girls Rock!—a group for teenagers—cool!

I keep scrolling and find a dozen texts asking for interviews. *Interviews? How do folks find my number?*

I think again. I'm gonna let Dad handle all that. He won't allow it, I know.

And the pictures! Seems like half of Cincinnati was walking around near Graeter's on Saturday, and apparently, they all captured it on their phones! Dozens of people have sent in photos and videos, the story says. There are dozens of photos of Darren on the ground covered by police—from different angles. My head starts spinning.

There's also a horrible school picture of me—where did they find that?

And a snapshot of me . . . lying on the ground—is that gooey spot *blood* on my arm? I stare and stare. How can that be *me*?

I don't even know how to feel about all this. Embarrassed? Maybe. Ashamed? Yeah, but I'm not sure why. And mad. *MAD!* And I don't know what to do with *any* of it.

We seem to be the horror story of the day. Guns. Police. Violence in the street and stuff. Lots of articles and editorials about racial profiling. A couple of articles talk about Darren and his superstar high school career—his college possibilities. There are a couple of mentions about me and the piano recital, but mostly they show that photo of me and the blood.

I wonder what Madame Rubenstein thought when I didn't show up. I'm sorry I disappointed her. And I'm really bummed I didn't get to play my sonatina. But all I really want is to go home. I don't even care which one.

CHAPTER 76
Exchange Day

AT EXACTLY 3:00 p.m., the four parents and Darren walk into my room. It's freaky. I'm usually at the mall being switched at this time. So I just pretend to be asleep.

"Should we wake her?" Mom whispers.

"She's had such a rough time—let her rest," Anastasia replies.

"Too bad this ice cream is gonna melt," I hear Darren say.

I pop my eyes open.

"I knew you were faking!" Darren hoots, his voice all high and happy.

"Where's my ice cream?" I demand. I cross my arms against my chest—gently.

"I'll run out and get a whole pint for you later on," he promises.

Mom holds a Target bag in her hand—that means fresh clothes. Maybe even new.

I catch her eye and mouth, "Thanks, Mom." I can't wait to change.

Both Dad and John Mark are wearing the same yummy man cologne. It's a little overpowering as they lean over me to kiss my head.

Anastasia reaches over and smooths my blanket, kinda like a mom would do.

Mom must have taken a quick shower when she went home, because her hair is still damp. She's wearing a T-shirt with purple sparkles that says, "My Other Car Is a Unicorn."

I watch a lot of hospital dramas on television, and this is the part where patients just want everybody to leave them alone. It's all going just a little too well. No arguments. No fights. No snippy remarks. Nothing. If they leave now, nothing bad can happen.

Dad clears his throat. Uh-oh. Here it comes.

"Uh, Nicole, I want to say something—in front of our daughter."

I tense up. Waiting for the arguments to kick in.

Dad continues. "I just want to offer my congratulations to you and John Mark about your upcoming nuptials. John Mark is a top-notch guy—and I can tell he loves my baby girl. I sincerely hope you'll both be very happy."

I'm for-real shocked. That was awfully nice.

Mom, who I think is just as surprised, replies, "Thank you, Isaiah. Really. Truly. I thank you." She looks at both of them. "And I also really wish the best for you and Anastasia on your wedding as well. I think all of us deserve a little happiness."

Well, slap me silly! They're honestly being nice to each other! Of course, if this were one of those Hallmark movies, one of them would then say, "Izzy's happiness comes first," then they'd all wait till I was grown and gone before they all got hitched. Ha! That's for sure not happening!

Well, at least they're not brawling over my bed. 'Cause it coulda gone that way too.

CHAPTER 77
Mom's Week

IT'S MONDAY. I'm feeling almost okay. They're gonna let me go home this afternoon. Mom is so psyched.

And get this: Dad even tells her if I need an extra week for her to take care of me, it would be okay. Whoa! That's pretty huge. My wall calendar will have to be re-done.

Madame Rubenstein stopped by last night. She stood by my bed and said Pianopalooza was meaningless without me. I gotta admit, that made me feel good, even if it wasn't true.

She brought me a copy of the recital program. And

there was my name, just as I'd always dreamed—in fancy script letters—*Isabella Badia Thornton*. This was rock-star stuff!

Then Madame Rubenstein started crying. *What?*

She found a tissue and smiled at me while she wiped her nose. Then she told me she was entering me in another recital—simply called Musical Overtures. It's later in the summer—for the more accomplished students, she told me. That's gonna be cool. Though maybe I'll skip the ice-cream run this time! Ha!

Imani's mom peeks in right after lunch, with both Heather and Imani. At first they were whispering and not really looking at me—I guess hospitals are pretty intimidating. That's a pretty good Kazilly word.

"Hey, girl. You okay?" Heather finally asks.

"Well, the room service is great!" I joke. "Three meals a day, with a lovely dessert cup of pills!"

"Does it hurt?" Imani asks.

I look directly in her eyes. "It hurts on the inside."

She nods at me knowingly. "I feel you."

They bring me up to date on what the rest of the kids were saying, and how the whole situation had kinda hit the Internet. I'm blown away.

They stay for twenty minutes or so. Imani tells me that Logan has been suspended from school for a couple of weeks. "And his mom is making him go to therapy," she adds.

"Good! He needs as much as he can get," I say, and we both nod in understanding.

Then, just before they leave, Heather hands me two little Tupperware containers of slime—one orange and one shiny silver. Now, *that* makes me feel normal! I can't wait to get back into making it myself.

I lay my head back on the pillow—it only hurts a little now—and close my eyes. Faint music is playing over a hospital speaker. I recognize it—"Für Elise," by Beethoven. I can play that one. I dance my fingers in the air.

Faster.

Slower.

Bass.

Treble.

Delicate.

White keys.

Black keys.

Blended perfectly.

AUTHOR'S NOTE

The Clementi piece Isabella performs in the novel is called Sonatina in C Major, op. 36, no. 1.

And in case you're interested, here's a link to hear the song played really, really well:

https://www.youtube.com/watch?v=0_Ksi2qmW0A

And PS, I can still play that piece!

ACKNOWLEDGMENTS

I would like to thank the following people:

—Janell, for your loving wisdom and enduring friendship.

—Makeda, for being the strong, unflappable sister, daughter, and survivor that you are.

—AJ, for being such a cool brother, and for surviving that scene at the end in real life!

—Crystal, for being the supermom whose love and strength make it all work.

—And Caitlyn, whose wisdom, knowledge, love, and fine-toothed, legendary green-pen edits make everything sing!